DATE DUE

0·00	Cr	R·00	Rc-N
C·00			gc11·00
			Cu
			eN

W9-DDR-078

DEMCO

THE TROUBLE
WITH
RAINBOWS

THE TROUBLE WITH RAINBOWS

•

Susan Aylworth

AVALON BOOKS
NEW YORK

PRINTED IN THE UNITED STATES OF AMERICA
ON ACID-FREE PAPER
BY HADDON CRAFTSMEN, BLOOMSBURG, PENNSYLVANIA

For Cathryn Hepburn, who told me Angelica wanted a book;
For Veronica Mixon, who kept this book alive;
And always, for Roger

Chapter One

*S*pring, *and a young man's fancy turns to thoughts of love—and young men aren't the only ones,* Angelica DeForest thought as she sat in the large bay window off her living room, watching the schoolkids walk by, many of them in pairs. The couple passing her window right now—probably no older than thirteen or fourteen—were adorable together, swinging their linked hands between them and smiling shyly, the girl giggling at something the boy had said. *They're so sweet,* Angelica thought with uncharacteristic longing. *If only . . .*

Now where did that come from? she chided herself, turning away from the window. If anyone had asked, she'd have testified that she'd long since given up the "if only's" and the dreams of what might have been, of what never would be if she didn't get her act together—and quickly. *It's time,* Angelica, she warned herself

1

sternly. *Unless you want to spend the rest of your life alone, it's time and past time.*

She needed to reorganize her life, to become bolder in going after what she wanted, to make new plans for the future, then make those plans come true. *But The Big Change will have to wait a little longer*, she thought with a sigh. It was almost time for her students to start arriving.

She started for the piano, planning to dust before her first afternoon lesson, but was interrupted by the telephone. "Hello?"

"Angelica? It's Cretia Carmody. Do you have a moment?"

"Yes, of course." She couldn't help wondering why Cretia had become so chatty lately. She'd hardly bothered to speak to Angelica during their school years. True, she was several years younger and had been a freshman when Angelica was a senior, but . . . "Sorry. What was that? I'm afraid I was, uh, distracted."

"I asked if you ever teach violin lessons," Cretia said.

"No, I never have. I have a couple of viola students, and several in beginning piano. But not violin. Why?"

"My niece wants to take lessons. Do you know anyone who teaches?"

"Locally, you mean? Here in Rainbow Rock?" Angelica combed her memory. "No, I can't think of anyone in this area, or Holbrook, either—not for private lessons." She paused. "I didn't know you had a niece here."

"I don't—yet," Cretia answered. "My brother Joe has accepted a job at the power plant. He's going to move his family here in a couple of weeks, as soon as they finish their school year. His daughter's eleven. She's taking violin lessons now and she's worried that she may not be able to continue when they move."

"Oh, I'm sorry. I'll keep my ear to the ground. If I hear of anyone, I'll let you know."

"Angelica?"

"Yes?"

"Is it possible you could consider taking *one* violin student? I know it's different from the viola, but it isn't *that* different, is it?" Cretia sighed. "I don't mean to push. It's just that I haven't found anyone who teaches locally, and it means so much to Victoria. Her mother played violin."

Angelica tried to keep the exasperation out of her voice. "Then perhaps her mother could teach her?" The silence on the other end of the line was a clue that she'd made some kind of faux pas. *The story of my life.* Angelica sighed. She'd never been good at social contacts.

"Her mother died," Cretia said. "Just over a year ago. Victoria is studying violin in her mother's memory."

"Oh. I'm sorry." *How do I always stumble into these things?* "I'm so sorry, Cretia. I didn't . . . I never would have . . ."

"It's okay. You had no way of knowing."

"But you're right, you know. The violin isn't really that different from the viola. . . ." Five minutes later, having committed herself to taking her first and only violin student, Angelica hung up the phone just in time to welcome her first piano student for the afternoon. *How do I get myself into these things?* she pondered again as little Rodney Chapman sat down to mangle "Row, Row, Row Your Boat" in the key of C.

*   *   *

"Well, what do you think?" By now the kids had had plenty of time to examine their new digs in Rainbow Rock, Arizona. This picturesque little town was where he had spent his own teen years, and Joe Vanetti was hoping for a little approval from the next generation. He'd certainly put the effort into making this work: paying extra for the moving crews to haul everything out and set it all up while he took Victoria and Nicholas to Southern California theme parks for three days; faxing his sister, Cretia, a detailed map of their rental home, drawn to scale, showing where everything should go so it could all be neatly put away before he and the kids arrived; labeling all the boxes to match the diagram. . . .

"It's fine, Dad." Victoria offered him the same dispirited, who-cares voice she'd been using for more than a year now.

"I like *my* room," Nicholas said, glancing at his dad to get official parental notice of the way he was one-upping his sister. "I've got a cool sliding glass door that leads out onto the patio."

"And which you are not to use after bedtime," his father said firmly.

"But Da-ad," Nicholas began.

"Quit while you're ahead, Nicholas," Joe warned him. "You could end up in Victoria's room, the one with the built-in vanity."

"Oh, goody." Nicholas rolled his eyes.

"I think I'll keep the vanity, Dad—if it's all the same to you." Victoria stared at her feet, drawing shapes on the floor with her toe.

She doesn't want me to know she cares, Joe noticed. *Poor kid. She's been a wreck since her mother died. And she's growing up. She needs her mother.* "Okay, honey," he said aloud. "That's where we'll keep you—for now, anyway." He grinned at her and ruffled her hair. She gave him her long-suffering look and combed her hair back into place with her fingers. *Yeah. That went over great.*

"So," he said, "since everything's all set up here, what d'ya say we call up your Aunt Cretia and her family and invite them to meet us for dinner? I hear there's a nice Thai place in Holbrook."

"Thai?" Nicholas wrinkled his nose. "Nobody should ever have to eat coconut milk with lime juice in it."

"You like the silvery rice noodles," Joe reminded, but Nicholas just turned up his nose.

"I like Thai, Dad." Victoria stuck her tongue out at her brother.

"Thanks, honey." *Wouldn't you know it? The only sure way to get my daughter to agree with me is if she can rub it in her brother's face.* "I'll call Cretia and Max and the gang. Maybe they'd like to meet us there."

Well, it's hardly an auspicious beginning, Joe concluded as he started for the phone, *but we're here. That's something.* As Victoria and Nicholas began bickering in the background, he sighed. *Maybe that's the best we're going to do, for now.* He could only hope tomorrow would be brighter.

It's almost two o'clock. I hope he's punctual. Then again, he was always quick. Angelica grinned at her own little joke as she paced back and forth in front of her picture window. It still stunned her that she was awaiting the arrival of Joe Vanetti, the hottest athlete—and nicest young man—Rainbow Rock High School had ever produced. That she had worshiped him all through junior high and high school was one secret she'd never whispered to a soul, a secret she expected to carry to her grave. That he'd never known she was alive was obvious to anyone who'd gone to school with them both.

Who could blame him? she pondered as she glanced at the clock yet again. *He was the town's Golden Boy and I was the shy, awkward girl who made a fool of herself every time she spoke or moved. It wasn't exactly a match made in heaven. Besides, I was a junior when he was a senior, and nobody ever notices the younger kids.*

She'd certainly given him every opportunity to notice her. She felt her face warming slightly as she remembered some of those "opportunities" now. There was the time she'd been sitting in the bleachers watching him compete in the state Class A wrestling qualifiers, held in Rainbow Rock that year because the school had won the state title three years in a row. She'd just sat down with her hot dog and a can of soda when the sophomore boy in front of her had waved to one of Joe's teammates and smacked her right in the face—sending ketchup, mustard, and soda spraying in every direction and showering her in the process. She'd missed Joe's winning match while she was cleaning up.

Then there had been the sectional basketball championship. Joe had scored more than sixty points, including the last-second, three-point shot to win by one as the clock ran out. She had stood in the bleachers to shout encouragement and had taken a misstep, catching her toe in the crack and pitching forward. She'd landed practically in the lap of the senior class clown, who had made a quick, loud quip about how this was the only way any boy would ever hold Miss DeForestation. Everyone around them had hooted with laughter.

There had been hundreds of other opportunities for Joe to notice her; she had insisted on creating them. She always checked Joe's class schedule and organized her own so she would pass him in the hall at least four or five times a day. She had done so for all of their years in the same school. She had gone to every game or match he ever played in, unless she had a conflict where she had to play viola for something. She'd even pushed herself to qualify for higher math classes, just so she could be in the same class with Joe—and she hated math.

She'd all but made a nuisance of herself, following Joe Vanetti around, hoping he'd notice her. *It might have worked, too, if I'd been more the noticeable type*, she reflected. But shy wallflowers weren't noticeable, and Joe had occupied the rarefied world of sports awards, scholastic success, and popular people that had simply never admitted klutzes like her.

Throughout those high school years, there had been other boys who had interested her—crushes, really— though none of them had ever noticed her, either. But no one had kept her interest and brought her back, over and over again, the way Joe had done. Joseph Martin Vanetti was the one she had always adored from afar, the dream date she had idolized. What she had felt for him had been much more like hero worship than puppy love.

And now he's coming here. After all these years, the first time I bring Joe Vanetti to my house is when he's looking for an old maid music teacher to tutor his daughter. Angelica smiled at the irony.

Ah, if only I had the nerve. . . . But what was the point

in even considering it? She'd never managed the nerve before now. She pursed her lips and dusted while she waited for Joe to arrive.

Joe parked his car at the curb and double-checked the address. Funny, he thought. *I've known Angelica De-Forest for . . . what? Twenty years? Twenty-five maybe. And I've never been to her house before.* He recognized the place; it really hadn't changed from how he remembered it. He'd first noticed it when Angelica and her mother had moved in with Old Lady Lunsford, the woman half the people in town called Grandma Poppy. Angelica had lived there with her mother and grandmother all through her junior high and high school years. Then, according to Cretia, she'd come back to town after finishing her studies at Northern Arizona University to take care of her aging mother, and had stayed on alone since her mother's death. *That sounds like a lonely existence*, Joe thought with a shudder. If there was one thing Joe knew well, it was loneliness.

Well, time to bell the cat, or maybe the correct expression here is "face the music." Joe smiled at his own pun and wiped his hands on his slacks. He couldn't remember the last time he'd felt this nervous about meeting anybody. He couldn't imagine why he'd still feel so intimidated by Angelica DeForest, after all these years.

I never really figured out what there was about her, Joe pondered as he looked up at the big house. *She was just always so cool, so aloof, so . . . intimidating.* He'd noticed her the first time he ever saw her, standing in front of Rainbow Rock Junior High School on her first day of seventh grade. He, the experienced, upperclassman eighth-grader, had tried to impress her by commenting to some of the younger students about school procedure. Angelica had regarded him with her cool, Ice Queen stare and turned her head away, and he had gulped down the rest of his planned instruction together with the lump in his throat. With her huge, sky-blue eyes and waist-length, honey-colored hair, Angelica had always been a beauty, and Joe had noticed her—plenty.

But it wasn't exactly a match made in heaven. Joe sighed, then noticed someone moving behind the front window. Was she waiting for him? *Whew! Better get my act together. I don't want her scolding me for being late.* Joe smiled wryly. Even now the thought of Angelica turning that icy blue stare on him could still give him the willies. No, there had never been much space for connections between Angelica DeForest and plain ol' Joe. She had occupied the rarefied world of classical music and formal recitals, and he was the commonest sort of guy, working his natural athletic ability into the hope of a scholarship. *Well,* he told himself again, *time to face the music.* Gathering a deep breath for courage, he strode up the walk and knocked on the front door of Poppy Lunsford's oh-so-perfect home.

Angelica opened the door to Joe's knock. "Mr. Vanetti," she said, waving him in.

"Angelica," he responded less formally. "I hope I'm not late."

"No, no," she said, flushing a bright rose color. She ducked her head. "Well, only a minute or two, perhaps."

She looked away, and Joe wondered why his lateness so embarrassed her, or if she was just embarrassed for him.

"Please come in and sit down," she offered, directing him toward the deep-red velvet love seat in the parlor.

"Thank you," he said, and sat.

Angelica remained standing. She looked so uncomfortable that Joe wondered what rules of etiquette he had violated. "Um, would you care for a glass of lemonade?" she asked, reaching for a tall, iced pitcher.

Joe wasn't thirsty, but he didn't want to offend this woman any further. Cretia had made it clear that Angelica was the only possibility for Victoria to have private violin lessons, unless he wanted to drive her all the way to Flagstaff—more than ninety miles. She'd also made it painfully clear that Angelica wasn't any too eager to take on his daughter's lessons. "Yes, I'd love some," he said, and waited while she poured. He noticed that she poured only one glass, leaving the other empty on the tray. "Thank you," he said as she handed him the glass. *Now, if I can just find a way to break the ice somehow. Of course, I never could through all those school years. . . .* No one broke through with the Ice Queen.

"Lucretia tells me you've moved back to stay," Angelica began as she took a seat, and Joe breathed a relieved sigh. *She* was breaking the ice.

"Yes, I've taken an engineering position at the power plant."

"At Cholla Lake, correct?"

Joe nodded. Locals often made a point of clarifying the closer plant, the one at Cholla Lake, from the larger Four Corners plant, though it was some distance away. "Yes, at Cholla Lake."

"She said you'd been working as an environmental engineer?"

"That's right, at a Southern California firm that specializes in environmental engineering."

"Just what is that?" Angelica asked.

Again Joe sighed in relief. He was on familiar territory here. "Our particular specialty was in managing large projects so they didn't have too great an impact upon the environment," he began. "If anyone needed to create a new landfill in the desert, we engineered it so there'd be no contamination of the local watershed. Once a copper mine near the Arizona border was applying for a permit to expand, and it was my job to be sure there'd be no heavy metals contamination of the local aquifers. That sort of thing." He shrugged, minimizing the importance of his work. "Our firm handled contracts throughout the western United States, but most of the work I did was in the Southwest: California, Arizona, Utah, Nevada . . . a few jobs in Oregon. Once I worked with a pineapple plantation in Hawaii."

"Oh?" Angelica looked at him with such rapt interest that he felt a little embarrassed for rambling on like this, but so flattered by her attention that he couldn't seem to quit.

"Yeah. The plantation owner wanted to dig a reservoir to preserve rainwater for the dry cycles. Some of the locals feared that digging where he wanted to, near the top of an old volcano, would anger Pele, and she'd bring the old volcano back to life. It was my job to help him find an appropriate place for the reservoir that wouldn't make the goddess angry."

"How did you do that?" Angelica asked quietly.

"I just helped him find a good place for a reservoir that wasn't on the volcano. It turned out that when I ran some tests on the place where he had originally planned to dig, I discovered he was working over an earthquake fault. If he had placed the reservoir there, there was a chance the pressure of the water on that fault might have caused some trouble. Maybe he'd have awakened ol' Pele after all." He grinned.

"Your work sounds fascinating," Angelica said, joining him in a smile. "And what will you do at Cholla Lake?"

"The same kinds of things, really, just here instead of all around. I'll be responsible for guaranteeing that our smokestack emissions comply with E.P.A. regulations, that the water our boilers emit into the lake isn't too hot to endanger fish or waterfowl, that the lake and the area around it meet state standards for a wetlands refuge. . . . That sort of thing."

"It sounds important," Angelica said, and again Joe felt that odd sensation of boyish pride that someone like Angelica would approve of him.

"Maybe not so important," he answered, "but necessary."

"I still say it's important work," Angelica answered, lowering her lashes.

Joe wondered what to say next, and where they were to go from here.

"So your daughter is studying violin?" Angelica asked, and again Joe blessed her for keeping the conversation going. He certainly didn't seem to be very good at it.

"Yes, she's been playing for three years, and her teachers in California felt she was making good progress. I'm afraid I wouldn't know, myself." This was one arena where Joe always felt out of his depth.

"You realize I've never taught violin. . . ."

"I know. I also know you're our best hope of continuing these lessons. I can't tell you how grateful I am that you're even willing to consider this. It means so much to Victoria."

"That's what your sister was telling me." Angelica gave him a small, sad smile. "So. Most of my lessons end with the school year at the end of May and start up again in the fall. Is that what you were planning on?"

"I don't want to disrupt your schedule," Joe began, "but Victoria is always so busy during the school year, she likes to catch up with her violin during the summer. I've been hoping you'd start her this week."

Angelica blushed again—a deep rose—color and looked away. "Oh. Well, I hadn't considered—"

"Of course, if that won't work for you, I can let her know you'll start in the fall," Joe offered. He didn't want to blow Victoria's chances.

"No, no. I can take her once a week. There will be a two-week hiatus when I plan to be away. That's the first two weeks in August. Other than that, it should work fine. Say, Wednesdays?"

"Wednesdays sound good."

After that things moved quickly. They agreed on an early afternoon hour and a price both considered fair. The only awkward moment came when Joe offered his hand as a way of shaking on the deal. Angelica hesitated just a moment too long, and Joe wondered if maybe his hand wasn't clean, or whether there was some rule of etiquette he didn't know.

Angelica was blushing slightly as she held out her hand. He noticed it shook just a little as he reached to take it. Immediately a shock sparked between them and he pulled away.

"Sorry," he said.

Angelica's rosy blush deepened, and she dropped her lashes toward the floor. "It's static," she said. "This old carpet . . . I'm sorry. I should have—"

He reached and took her hand again. This time there was no shock, but there was an odd, familiar warmth. Angelica noticed it, too. Her sky-blue eyes opened wide and her lips parted slightly, as if she was about to speak. She closed her lips instead.

The moment passed, and Joe reluctantly let go of Angelica's hand. "I'll see you next Wednesday, then," he said.

He's hardly changed at all, Angelica observed as she watched Joe walk to his car. *His hair is showing a bit of gray at the temples, and he's wider in the chest and shoulders. Other than that, he could practically be the same young man who walked out of Rainbow Rock High School on graduation night some seventeen years ago.* Then, *No,* she corrected herself. *Two other things have changed as well. There's that sense of deep sadness that hovers about him like a cloud. Then there's also the way he seemed so tongue-tied. I remember Joe as being ever so confident, always in charge. Imagine me being the one to make conversation!*

That was one for the record books. She'd hardly had a clue what to say to him. Luckily she'd remembered her Aunt Lucia once advising her cousin Heidi: "If you don't know what to say to a man, you can always ask him about his work. Men love to talk about their work." Well, his work and his daughter had been the subjects that had gotten Angelica through that difficult interview. She sighed, sinking into a window seat to watch as Joe drove away. Simple conversations like that seemed to be so easy for other people. *What's the matter with me?* Angelica wondered for the umpteenth time. That she wasn't like other people was obvious to anyone who knew her. What to do about it seemed to elude them all.

"Hi, folks. Anybody home?" Joe entered the Carmody house by way of the kitchen door.

"Hi, Dad. We're in here," Nicholas called from the living room.

Joe wound his way through the halls to find his son and daughter spread out on the living room floor, each with a video controller, each doing his or her part to save the earth from conquering aliens while their cousins Lydia and Danny, and Max's daughter Marcie, all cheered and rooted for the forces of Good.

"Hi, Uncle Joe." Lydia looked up as he entered.

"Hi there, cupcake." He ruffled Lydia's hair. Instead of the long-suffering look he usually got from his own daughter, his niece gave him a wide grin. "Is your mom around?"

"Yeah. I think she's in the laundry room."

"Thanks," he answered and headed down the hall. "Cretia?" he said as he reached the laundry room, announcing himself so he didn't startle her.

"Oh hi, Joe. How was your meeting with Angelica?"

"Okay, I guess." He leaned against the doorjamb. "It's funny. I never know what to say to her. She always seems so above the rest of us."

Cretia turned with a wise smile. "Maybe she only *seems* that way."

Joe furrowed his brow. "What are you getting at?"

Cretia shrugged. "It's hard to know what's going on in someone else's head, isn't it? I mean, sometimes you get this sense that another person is just so superior, when really all—"

"I'm not good at riddles." Joe frowned in impatience. "Why don't you just say what you mean?"

"I mean that throughout high school I always thought Angelica was just feeling superior. You know, haughty, conceited. We used to call her stuck-up."

Joe looked thoughtful. "Yeah, I remember. What most of the kids said about her wasn't even that nice."

Cretia nodded. "I know. But I don't think *she* thought of herself as superior."

"Yeah, I know what you mean." Then Joe frowned again. "Or maybe I don't. What exactly is your point?"

"I don't think Angelica ever meant to be cold, or distant, or intimidating. I think she's just shy, and maybe a little socially inept. She spent all her life with older people and was never around other kids very much. By the time she got to be high school–aged, she didn't know how to talk to anyone but adults. I suspect she'd have loved to, if she'd only known how."

Joe rubbed his forehead. "I never thought of that."

Cretia smiled and put a load of whites in the washer. "How did she look?" she asked.

"Great, just great," Joe said, thinking inwardly that her appearance had only improved since high school. He'd always thought her beautiful—as beautiful and as thoroughly unapproachable as an ice sculpture. Honey-colored hair that had once brushed her waistline now turned under just below her shoulders. Those huge, ice-blue eyes still beckoned from under long, deep-brown lashes. Even her blush was lovely—never ruddy, but a more rosy color that emphasized her high, wide cheekbones, small, straight nose, and delicate mouth. She was as tall as he had remembered, probably at least five-eight, and, though slim, she'd grown into a woman's shape, nicely rounded in all the right places. "She looked great," he said again, missing the speculative look his sister was giving him.

Joe looked up. "I didn't think to ask. You aren't usually home at this time of the afternoon, are you?"

"No, not usually, but Kurt is shooting an interview in the studio this evening, so I'll need to be over at Rainbow Productions for a couple of hours later. I thought I'd scoot home and run some wash before I get dinner on the table. That will make things easier when the kids are looking for clean clothes tomorrow."

Joe took a quick look around. "You seem to have things well in hand here," he said.

Cretia smiled. "That's thanks to Max. As soon as we were married, he insisted on hiring a housekeeping service. They come every Tuesday morning and do all the heavy cleaning. He also hired a service to clean carpets, and another that does windows. With him working nearly full-time in his new machine shop and me putting in full-time hours at the studio, it seemed necessary to have help."

"Well, I'd say you're managing beautifully." Then he carefully softened his expression. "And you really seem happy in your new marriage," he said. "You and Max and the kids make a nice family."

"Thank you." Cretia added a fabric softener sheet to

the load in the dryer and turned it on. "We are happy. And you're right that remarriage has been just what I needed. You know, the time may be coming when you'll want to start thinking about that yourself."

"Oh, no. Don't even get started in that direction," Joe warned, suddenly wary. "A woman like Roberta simply can't be replaced. I don't even want to think about trying."

Cretia huffed, exasperated. "Nobody here is talking about replacing anybody," she said, speaking distinctly. "If I'd even *thought* of replacing my ex-husband, I'd have kicked myself all over the desert." She stepped closer and laid a gentle hand on Joe's arm. "Remarriage isn't about replacement, Joe. It's about finding someone else you can love, maybe not in the same way at all, but loving again, anyway. It's about forging new relationships and new partnerships and not being lonely anymore."

Joe pulled away, not willing to be snared in his sister's dream. "I'm glad it's working for you," he said.

"But that reminds me," Cretia went on, more businesslike now. "I'm planning a big barbecue this weekend to welcome you and your kids to town and to say goodbye to Marcie. She's going back to Southern California to spend some time with her mother before the new school year and she'll be flying out on Monday. So if you don't have other plans, can you and the kids come be our *other* guests of honor? It'll be Saturday evening, around sixish."

Plans? When do I ever have other plans? Joe thought wryly. Aloud, he answered, "Sure. Saturday evening sounds fine."

"I need to warn you that most of the people who'll be coming are married couples, some with children," Cretia began. "I don't think there will be any single adults here except you."

"That's okay. I'm getting used to it."

"But you might be more comfortable if you invite someone to join you." Cretia pressed on.

"Cretia, you know I don't know anybody here anymore. . . ."

"Then maybe you wouldn't mind if I invited Angelica?" she asked. "It would give her a chance to meet Victoria before they begin lessons together."

"Angelica?" Joe paused, remembering how she'd looked when their hands had touched just an hour ago and an idle spark had flown between them. "That might be a good idea—for her and Victoria to meet, I mean." Then he caught Cretia's eye. "Just let's not pretend it's a date or anything like that, okay? I mean, I'm not in the market for dating and I don't want anyone to get the wrong idea."

"You made that quite clear," Cretia said, her tone making it clear what she thought. "Maybe I'll ask her to play something for us."

"That would be nice," Joe said. He had never known much about music—not good music, anyway—but he had always enjoyed hearing Angelica play.

"Good. I'll give her a call," Cretia said.

Joe couldn't help noticing there was a twinkle in her eye as she said it.

I'll have to keep an eye on that meddling sister of mine, he thought as he walked back down the hall to gather up his children. *I don't want her thinking that just because she's happily remarried, she can make the same arrangements for me.* Still, he couldn't help thinking that it would be nice—very nice—to see Angelica DeForest again.

Chapter Two

Saturday evening, and I'm dressing to go out. Now that's something I don't do every week. So what do I wear? Do I even know what people wear to barbecues? Angelica stood in front of the full-length mirror in the room that had once been the maid's quarters. After her mother's death, she had taken this room so she could close off the "family wing" of the big house, reducing both her utility bills and the amount of space she needed to keep clean.

She lifted a blue dress in sand-washed silk out of her closet and held it in front of her. *If I were playing at a wedding, this would be great, but does anybody wear a silk dress to a barbecue?* She shook her head and hung the dress back in the closet, then found herself wishing she owned more slacks.

Slacks, or "trousers" as Grandma Poppy had called them, were men's clothing. That had been drummed into her throughout her young years. She could practically hear her grandmother saying, "Now dear, you can't expect a man to notice a woman who's dressed just like he is. Never wear trousers, darling. It's a mistake the young women of this generation just haven't come to recognize." Well, the young women of her generation had never yet come to recognize it, and all of them were married—except for Poppy Lunsford's granddaughter, who had never been allowed to wear slacks. *You were wrong about the slacks, Grandmother*, she whispered to Poppy's memory. *You may well have been wrong about a lot of things.*

Once, years ago, when she was away from home at N.A.U. and feeling a bit rebellious, she had actually spent a little of her own money—money she had earned from playing viola at a faculty reception—to buy a pair of blue jeans. She'd hidden them in the bottom drawers of her dresser or the back of her closet during the long years she had lived here with her grandmother and later, with her mother, knowing what kind of squawk she'd have to put up with if either of them ever saw her in anything so common as blue jeans. She wondered if there was any chance they'd fit her now.

Digging the jeans out of the back of her closet, she tried them on and was surprised to find they still fit just as they had when she first bought them, creating a lean, long profile that Angelica rather liked. Combined with a sparkling white silk shirt and a sky-blue "big shirt" in soft velour, they created an effect of casual elegance. *I'm wearing jeans tonight*, she whispered to her mother's memory. *You see, this time I'm a guest. It's true, they have asked me to play, but this is really all about meeting Victoria and getting to know her a little, so she won't feel so shy about coming for lessons. It's a kind of caring I could have used more of when I was her age.*

Enough of that, she warned herself. Feeling sorry for herself over her strange upbringing didn't do her any good, and it did nothing to help her cope with her memories of her two rather odd parents. *Face it,* she reminded herself. *You were a surprise baby, and a complication in their lives that neither of them had planned for. It wasn't their plan to become parents when they were old enough to be grandparents already, and they did the best they could with you, considering.*

"That's true," she said aloud, "but it didn't exactly make things easier on me, either, now did it?"

Feeling slightly disloyal to the memory of the three well-intentioned, though sometimes misguided, people who had raised her, Angelica slipped on a pair of leather sandals. Then she dressed up her casual ensemble with a silver neck chain and a pair of silver earrings, and even heightened her color with some eye makeup and a little rose-colored lipstick before picking up her viola case and starting for her car. "I'm going to have fun tonight," she murmured to her family ghosts. "If I can possibly manage it, I'm going to relax and have fun."

"Just have fun, honey. That's what this evening is all about." Joe smiled at his daughter as he opened the car door for her and directed her toward Cretia's backyard. Since her mother's death, Victoria had had trouble with crowds. Even a group as large as this family gathering, probably no more than thirty people altogether, could wilt his little darling, turning her into a shade-seeking violet. "Why don't you find Lydia and Danny and see what they're into?" he said, herding both Victoria and Nicholas in the direction of their cousins.

As much as he was willing to push Victoria, the fact was, he knew exactly how she felt. People demanded energy. Being sociable with more people demanded more energy, and since Roberta had vanished from their lives, none of them had any energy to spare. Sometimes he even wondered if he had enough to get out of bed in the morning. If it hadn't been for the kids, who needed him more now than ever, he suspected he might not have gotten up at all. He might have just stayed in bed, waiting for death to claim him, too.

It would have been easier, he thought with a sigh. Then, because death hadn't come yet, he pasted on the illusion of a happy face and went to meet the friends and family that Cretia had gathered in his honor.

"Look, everyone. Here's Joe!" Cretia called as Joe stepped into the yard, and a couple of dozen heads turned to greet him. He felt exhausted just looking at them all.

For the next few minutes, he made the rounds as his sister introduced him to one guest or another. Many, like Jim McAllister and Peggy Taylor—Jim's wife, now known as Meg—he remembered from his high school days where they had been in the class just younger than his. Others, like Jim's younger brothers, Kurt and Chris, he'd heard Cretia speak of often enough that he felt he knew them. Still others, like Kurt's wife, Alexa, were new to him, though he'd occasionally heard their names.

He walked around the yard, greeting them all, trying to make small talk and apparently managing it well enough that none of them suspected his heart wasn't in it. Then, with a start, he realized he'd been waiting for one introduction that hadn't happened yet. He turned toward his sister, wanting to ask if Angelica was coming after all, then decided against it, not wanting to give Cretia any ideas. *As if she doesn't have enough of her own*, he thought.

Still, he looked up every time the side gate opened, or someone stepped into the yard from the house. He'd been looking up for nearly half an hour when he saw the face he'd been looking for. Then, when he saw her, he almost dropped his jaw.

"Wow!" he mumbled aloud, then looked around to make sure no one had heard him. Thank goodness Cretia had gone to the door to welcome her latest guest. Apparently he'd gotten away with that little slip. Reminding himself to watch his reactions in the future, he started in their direction.

She looks fantastic, he thought as he made his way among the other guests. He couldn't remember ever seeing Angelica looking so relaxed. For that matter, he couldn't remember ever seeing her dressed casually. During their school years, he had occasionally wondered if she knew what "casual" meant. *Well, she knows now*, he decided with approval. The sky-blue shirt she was wearing brought out the blue of her eyes, making them look huge and lustrous, as if the whole sky resided there for all to see, and the blue jeans showed off her long, slim legs, giving her a young, coltish look.

Before he quite realized what he was doing, he stepped up next to Cretia and spoke to her guest. "I'm glad you could join us this evening."

Angelica smiled, and a bit of that rosy blush heightened the glow of her complexion. "I . . . I thought it would be a good chance to meet your daughter."

"Of course," Joe said easily. "I think she's in the side yard, with her cousins. If you'll come with me—"

"My viola." Angelica lifted the case. "Is there a safe place where I could put this down?"

"How about inside, on the dining room table?" Cretia offered. "Because we're eating outside, no one will be using that table. It should be perfectly safe there."

"Thank you." Angelica stepped back inside and emerged a moment later, her hands empty. "Well," she said, "Shall we meet Victoria?" She looked to Cretia when she said it.

Cretia shook her head. "I need to check the potatoes, but Joe can show you where the kids are."

"Sure," Joe said, quickly grabbing the opening his sister had created. "This way." He indicated the direction and Angelica fell into step beside him.

"I understand Max's daughter is leaving for the summer?" she asked.

"Yes. She's going to spend some time with her mother and stepfather in Orange County. Cretia invited some of her school friends to see her off."

"Orange County. That's where you just came from, isn't it?"

"That's right," Joe answered as they walked. "In fact, our place was only a few miles from where Marcie's mother lives."

Angelica stopped walking. "Why'd you come back, Joe? Weren't there more opportunities for your kids out there?"

Joe paused, too, but looked toward the side yard when he spoke. "That one is tough to answer. The question of opportunities kind of depends on which opportunities we're talking about."

"I was thinking of things like Victoria's violin lessons, and other sorts of lessons or clubs, sports groups—things like that."

"It's true, there are more of those kinds of opportunities out there. Victoria and her mother used to go to plays and concerts all the time. Sometimes I went with them; sometimes they just called it a 'girls' night out' and went by themselves. Nicholas was just getting old enough to go to a play once in a while when—" He cut himself off, looking away again. "But the kids have family out here, and that's something we didn't have enough of where we lived before."

He opened the gate into the side yard, where a dozen youngsters played on some swings and chin-up bars. "Victoria?" he called. "Come meet your new violin teacher."

A small, dark child separated herself from the crowd and came toward them. Joe couldn't help noticing what a contrast they made as his daughter stood opposite the tall woman who would be her teacher. About normal height for her age, Victoria was a full foot shorter than Angelica, and her olive complexion, dark eyes, and short-cropped, near-black hair were a startling contrast to Angelica's ivory skin, blue eyes, and long hair the color of spun gold.

"Victoria," he said formally, "this is Miss DeForest. She will be teaching your violin lessons."

"Miss DeForest," Victoria said, offering her hand.

Angelica shook it soberly. "If your father doesn't mind, you may call me Angelica," she said.

Woman and girl looked to Joe, who said, "If Miss DeForest doesn't mind, then Angelica is fine with me."

"Okay, Angelica," Victoria said.

"We'll start next Wednesday," Angelica said. "Be sure to bring your music with you so I can see what you are playing now, and of course, you'll need to bring your own violin. I think your father may have explained to you that I don't have one."

"I know," the child said. "You're a violist, right?"

"That's right." Angelica gave the child a sympathetic smile. "I know you probably didn't plan on taking violin lessons with a violist, but—"

"That's okay. I'm not very good yet. I'm sure you can still teach me a lot."

Angelica smiled, trying to hold back a chuckle as the child described so ably her opinion of violists without even realizing she did so. "I'll do my best," she offered.

Then Victoria turned to Joe. "Dad, may I be excused now?"

"Sure, honey." Victoria rejoined the group and Angelica watched from the sidelines, thinking how different her life might have been if she had ever been welcomed into a group the way Victoria was now. She couldn't remember ever fitting in so easily with that many children. She couldn't remember fitting in with children at all.

She slowly surveyed the group. "Let me guess," she said. "The little boy on the monkey bars is your son, right?"

Joe beamed. "Right, that's Nicholas. How did you know?"

Angelica smiled. "Isn't it obvious?"

When Joe looked, he decided it was. Nicholas was a smaller, male version of his sister with the same olive complexion, dark eyes, and thick, near-black hair.

"Yeah, I guess it is," he said. "What can I say? They got my coloring."

"I'd say so," Angelica answered, smiling wryly.

They turned back toward the barbecue, Joe closing the side gate behind them. "Looks like they're starting to bring the food out," he observed.

Angelica's mind was apparently elsewhere. "Joe?" she asked. "Your children are Victoria and Nicholas, right?"

"Right." He couldn't help wondering where this discussion was going.

"Did you ever consider calling them by nicknames? Like Vickie? Or Nick?"

He pursed his lips. "I wanted to," he said. "I thought we would when we chose such formal names for them. But Roberta, my wife, wouldn't hear of it. She said we had given them lovely names and that's what they would be called. Even when teachers or kids at school tried to shorten their names, Roberta insisted they be called Victoria and Nicholas. In fact, she never let me call her by a nickname, either. I teased her about that when we first started dating. I even tried out a few nicknames on her, like Berta or Robbie." Joe paused, his thoughts focused on that happy time, now so far away.

"I don't suppose she approved," Angelica offered.

"She about had a hissy fit," Joe admitted, remembering how livid Roberta had become. "She told me if I ever wanted to see her again, I'd call her Roberta and that would be that. Later, when she made the same decision about Victoria and Nicholas, I guess I was ready for it."

"My mother made that same decision," Angelica said quietly.

Joe returned from that distant world of memory, thinking instead of the real flesh-and-blood woman who stood beside him.

"I remember when I was in the second grade," Angelica said, "and all the children in my school class seemed to have nicknames except me. There was a Susan we called Susie, and a JoEllen we called Jo, and a Samantha whom everyone called Sammie. We even had a Donella we called Bootsie." She grinned. "I can't explain that one, so don't ask."

He smiled back. "Okay. I won't."

"Even the boys in my class were Bobby and Rick and Johnny," Angelica went on. "One day, when a classmate called me Angie, I was so delighted. I felt like I was finally one of the group."

Angie? he thought. *Angie. I can't imagine Angelica DeForest as an Angie.* Aloud he said, "I guess your mother didn't agree?"

"Not at all," Angelica responded. "She said that she and my father had given me a lovely name and I must never abuse it by allowing the children to refer to me by something so common and vulgar as 'Angie.' She made it sound like a swear word when she said it." Angelica sighed. "The next day I dutifully went back to school and told my classmates they were to call me Angelica, and nothing else."

"But it made you sad?"

"Almost heartbroken." Angelica offered a soft smile.

Joe held that smile like a wish, catching the expression on Angelica's lovely face and committing it to memory. Instead of lowering her lashes, she held his gaze. For a long moment, the two connected.

That was when Max called that the food was ready and everyone should gather near the grill for a blessing on their dinner. Reluctantly Joe turned away from Angelica, opened the gate, and called the children to join them while Max said grace. Then, to Angelica, he offered, "Let me walk you back to the food."

"Sounds good," she agreed. He offered his arm, and she took it.

As they walked side by side, Joe realized he had probably misinterpreted and misunderstood Angelica De-Forest worse than he had ever imagined. The thought that she had once wanted to be called Angie was amazing, most amazing indeed.

"Can I help you to some spareribs?" Max offered from his place at the grill.

"No, thank you." Angelica smiled to take the sting out of her rejection.

"Hamburger? Hot dog?" Max was selling hard.

"No, thanks," Angelica said again. "I'll just skip the meat course, if you don't mind."

"Vegetarian?" Joe asked.

She shook her head. "No, I like meat as much as the next guy, maybe more than most. But I find it doesn't like me very much. As a rule, I'm happier if I don't eat it often, maybe no more than once or twice a month."

"I've often wondered about that," Joe said. "I mean, I hear about people who are vegetarians or who, like you, just prefer not to eat much meat, and I wonder what they do eat. Can you help me out here?"

Angelica shrugged. "Pretty much what everybody else eats, I guess, just minus the meat." She showed him her plate. "I'm filling up on the roasted potatoes and onions, the green salad, the broccoli-and-carrot dish, fresh corn. . . . See? Everything's here but the meat."

"Hmm," Joe said. "I see. It doesn't look like a bad meal, just . . . incomplete."

Angelica smiled. "For you, maybe. For me, it's all I need."

"But you do eat meat sometimes?"

"Sure, though I tend to save that for when I eat out. That way I can just microwave a potato or steam some vegetables and dinner's ready quickly." She shrugged. "I do occasionally cook meat, but more often than not, I'll scramble some eggs or make an omelet for my main course, if I don't just choose the potatoes or rice and veggies."

"That sounds interesting. I think I might like to get some recipes from you," Joe said. "It would probably be good for the kids and me if we ate less meat, and I'm not much of a cook as it is."

"It's true that most Americans could get by on a lot less meat than we eat," Angelica said, choosing to ignore his comment about not being much of a cook. Then a bold idea occurred to her. Really bold. Too bold, maybe. But hadn't she determined to be more bold? Even when she'd seen the kids walking by her house in pairs just last week, she'd told herself it was about time she stuck her neck out a little.

So, okay, I'm going for it, she told herself. Then, before she could be frightened into ignoring the impulse, she spoke. "Maybe sometime you and your children could join me for a meatless meal at my house," she said.

When Joe looked surprised, she hurried on. "I could cook the sorts of foods I cook when I'm trying to avoid meat, with maybe a nice egg casserole or quiche as a main dish, and if you and the kids all liked it, I could share the recipe with you after." She felt that infernal, ever-present blush rising and looked away, hardly able to believe she had actually invited Joe Vanetti to eat at her home. She dared to glance at him and saw him looking as surprised as she felt. "Of course, if you'd rather not . . ."

"No, no. I'd love . . . we'd love to come," Joe said. "It would be good to, you know, try the food out on the kids first, just to see what they thought of it. So, uh, when?"

"When?" Angelica repeated.

"Yeah. When do you want us to come over?"

Angelica, who had acted on the idea without really thinking it through, was uncertain now about how to follow up. "Oh, uh, is there any time that's particularly good for you?"

"Like I said . . ." Joe shrugged. "I'm not a good cook at the best of times. Just about any evening we'd be grateful for something I didn't have to battle into submission before it got to the table."

Angelica chuckled. Emboldened by the fact that he had said yes to her first proposal, she chose an early time. "How about tomorrow after church?" she asked. "If you don't already have other plans . . ."

"I'm afraid we do."

Joe looked so uneasy that Angelica felt certain he'd accepted her original offer only to be polite. "That's okay. If you'd really rather not come . . ."

"No! I want . . . I mean, we want to come. How about Monday?" he asked. "It's my first full day of work and I'd be grateful if I didn't have to try to scrape up a meal when I get home. How does that work with your schedule?"

"Let's see, let me think," Angelica said, stalling for time. *If I add up everything on my schedule for the next three months, I probably have a whole week's worth of busy little things to keep me occupied.* "Yes, I think Monday will be fine."

"Well, okay then. Monday it is. We usually try to eat around six. Is that okay with you?"

"Six will be fine," Angelica assured him.

Joe looked toward his daughter. "Oops. Looks like Victoria has decided she'd rather tease her brother than fill her own plate. If you'll excuse me?"

"Certainly." Angelica nodded as he put down his plate and walked toward his squabbling children.

Let's see now, did I just invite Joe Vanetti to have dinner at my house? she asked herself, then answered, *Yep, I think I really did. Wow. I wonder if this means we're dating?* Again she answered her own question. *No, of course not. This is more like the time I had my married friend, Cassandra, over, along with her husband and kids. This is just entertaining a friend, that's all. It doesn't count as dating unless it's just the two of us, right?*

At a loss to keep answering her own questions, she made a note about dinner Monday and tucked it into her purse. Date or no date, she was going to make sure to have everything as nice as possible when Joe Vanetti came to her home Monday evening.

Joe sat entranced, magically stirred and soothed by the lovely Mozart piece Angelica was playing. But the music was only one of the miracles before him. Angelica herself was a vision, passionate in her interpretation of the elegant phrases. He wondered how he ever could have found her icy.

Did I really just agree to have dinner with Angelica Monday night? Joe asked himself, amazed. *Yes. Yes, I think I did. Wow.* He paused in his self-discovery to appreciate her expert technique as Angelica executed a delicate arpeggio. *Amazing*, he thought again.

Later, he walked through his sister's yard, still deeply moved by the music, and by what he had discovered about the musician. He paused as he saw his son go by, insisting that Nicholas have something for seconds besides three hamburgers, two hot dogs, and a slab of spareribs. As he looked at that plate, he couldn't help wondering what Nicholas would think of Angelica's meatless Monday.

So, does this mean we're dating? he asked himself, following with a quick answer. *No, no, not at all. This is just like having dinner here tonight, just as if Max and Cretia were inviting us over again, that's all. It's just a friend having the family to dinner. It wouldn't count as a date unless it was just the two of us, with no kids around. Right?* Not having anyone else around to answer his question, he pretended he hadn't asked it, and scribbled a note to himself so he wouldn't forget Monday evening. *As if that was a real risk*, his thoughts quietly teased him.

"We're often told that the purpose of the parables is for us to abstract them, to take a major principle from them and apply it in our own lives." Reverend Phelps was at the pulpit and Angelica sat half-listening. The other half was focused on the little family group sitting a few rows in front and to the right, next to Max and

Cretia Carmody. Marcie Carmody, who wouldn't fly out until tomorrow, was still with them today, and the kids had formed a family patchwork down the aisle: Max and Cretia at one end with Victoria and Lydia beside them, then Marcie on the other side of Lydia, then Danny and Nicholas, with Joe as the other bookend. They were an attractive family, if somehow incomplete.

"A close reading of the parable of the prodigal teaches us much more about the quality of forgiveness," the minister went on. "We learn about the experience of seeking forgiveness, or of forgiving others, only when we put ourselves into the shoes of the various characters, experiencing the pain of the prodigal when he realized he was alone in the world and had already burned the bridges that connected him to his family."

Angelica thought about burned bridges, and about all the times she would have liked to have burned the bridges, or at least some of them, that connected her to her peculiar family. She had been faithful to those connections, often at the expense of herself. As the minister talked on, it occurred to her that maybe she was more like the unforgiving brother, finding it hard to let go of some of the resentment her family situation had forced on her over the years.

The minister went on while Angelica pondered the inadvertent wrongs done by her well-meaning parents. *They never meant to hurt me. They didn't realize they were making me a social misfit.*

"We must learn to seek forgiveness as the prodigal did. So we must also learn to feel forgiveness. Such was the lesson taught to the other son, the faithful one."

The faithful one. Was that a fair description of what she had been during all those years she'd stayed at home, tending her dying grandmother, then her own aging mother, while others of her generation played and loved and built lives for themselves? And didn't she have plenty of resentment for the opportunities she had lost in being "faithful"? Would she ever be able to go on, grow, and make something of her life if she couldn't let go of the hurts from her past?

"Maybe it's time," she whispered, resolving to let go and move on. She couldn't help it that her eyes, and her thoughts, strayed to the pew in front of her, strayed to Joe Vanetti. She didn't dare to dream that moving on might include Joe, but as she watched him, he turned to meet her eyes. Though her temptation was to look away, she held his gaze instead, and was pleased when he returned her smile.

"Dad, will you read me a story?" Nicholas was settled in bed, and by now should probably have been asleep.

"What's going on here, big guy?" Joe asked. "You haven't had bedtime stories for a couple of years now."

"Yeah, I know. I just thought, maybe tonight . . ."

It was Sunday evening, and the day had been rough for them all—adjusting to church in a new place, then the dinner at Max and Cretia's house, then a rougher-than-usual evening at home, complete with children bickering and Dad laying down the law. It wouldn't hurt too much to relent a little on a story, would it?

"Tell you what, Nicholas. What if I retell a story from the Bible? Something we heard in church today?"

"Well, okay," Nicholas agreed reluctantly, and Joe related the story of the prodigal, trying to embellish with detail and enliven with inflection so it would seem more exciting for an eight-year-old. All the while he was thinking about the principle of forgiveness and how important it can be, especially when dealing with family. When an image of his in-laws popped into mind, he firmly ordered it away.

Nicholas was nodding off as he finished the story, and he kissed his son good night. Then, almost to the door, he turned back, thinking of what Angelica had asked him yesterday.

"Nicholas?"

"Yeah, Dad."

"Have you ever wanted to be called Nick?"

The boy was slow in answering. "Yeah, I used to," he said, "especially when I first started school and some of the guys there wanted to call me Nick. When I asked Mother about it, she . . . well, she didn't like that idea."

"Yeah, I know what you mean," Joe agreed, still stung by hearing his late wife referred to as Mother.

He and Roberta had argued about that when the babies were little. It was only because he insisted upon it that she had ever allowed the children to call him anything but Father. Formal or not, he had liked the idea of someone calling him Dad. He had insisted on it over her objection, but had never been able to get her to back down when she insisted equally stubbornly on being called Mother.

"You know, Nick," he said carefully, enunciating each word. "It wouldn't hurt too much if you wanted to be called Nick now."

"You don't think it would be . . . bad? To do something Mother wouldn't have wanted?"

"No, son." Joe bit his lip. "In this case, I don't think it would be bad at all." He stepped into the hall. Just before he closed Nick's door, he whispered, "Remember your prayers . . . Nick."

"I will," the boy answered. "Thanks, Dad."

Since he already felt as if someone was wringing his heart, Joe stepped down the hall to look in on his daughter.

"Victoria?" he asked. "Are you still awake?"

"Yes, Dad."

"Can I ask you something?"

"Sure," she answered, her voice dreamy with sleep.

"Have you ever wanted to be called Vickie?"

There was a long pause, and Joe wondered if his daughter had nodded off. "Can I tell you the truth?"

"Of course," he answered, hoping he didn't sound as annoyed to his daughter as he did to himself.

"I never wanted to be called Vickie," she said, "but when I was younger, I used to think it would be really cool to be called Tori."

"Tori?" Joe could feel his eyebrows rising.

"Yeah. You know, like Tori Amos?"

"Um, yeah," Joe answered. *No, actually, can't say that I do.* "Tori Amos, huh?"

"Yeah. I used to think that would be really cool."

"Victoria?"

"Yeah, Dad."

"We can call you Tori now, if you'd still like that."

"Really?"

Joe gulped. *Tori. That will take some getting used to.* "Yeah, baby. Really. If that's what you want."

"Yeah. I think that'd be great."

"Then Tori it is. Good night, hon."

"Goodnight, Daddy," his daughter, Tori, answered.

I don't remember the last time she called me Daddy,

Joe thought. Then, *Oh, yes I do. She was probably about five and her mother chewed her out for it, told her she wasn't a baby anymore and she should stop the baby talk.*

Ouch. The memory hurt. Did it indicate something about his mourning process that he was beginning, once in a while, to remember that his late wife hadn't always been perfect? That once in a while, even *she* could have blind spots? That now and then, she made mistakes?

He turned toward his own bed, exhausted, and prepared for an early night's sleep. He had his first day on a new job coming up tomorrow and he hadn't done that in . . . how many years?

As he prepared himself for rest, he couldn't help thinking gratefully of Angelica DeForest and the one little thing their conversation yesterday had taught him. If nothing else came of his meeting her again, if the children didn't like her meatless cooking, and Victoria—no, Tori—didn't learn violin from her the way she'd hoped, if nothing else happened that made their meeting worthwhile, she had already helped him overcome an important barrier that had separated him from his children, without his even realizing it. In future years, he would be closer to Tori and Nick because of something Angelica had taught him, and that was worth a lot.

Joe smiled as he crawled into bed. He was thinking of Angelica, anticipating their evening together tomorrow, when he drifted off to sleep.

Chapter Three

Angelica buzzed around her kitchen, creating a veritable hive of nervous activity. She couldn't remember when she had ever fussed over the details of a meal the way she did now. Would the kids like cucumber in the salad? Would they eat fresh tomatoes? If she made the egg casserole with green chilies in it, would *anyone* eat it, other than herself? How many vegetable dishes should she plan? She finally decided she was going to prepare what her instincts told her would go over best, leave lots of options available, and keep her fingers crossed.

She began in the early afternoon with the baking. Her mother had taught her always to bake from scratch, so she started her walnut-wheat loaf by chopping two cups of fresh walnuts. While the bread was rising, she grated cheddar and jack cheese for the *chili relleno* casserole. Then she gave the front rooms of the house a thorough cleaning and ventured into the garden for fresh vegetables and flowers. As a final touch, she went into Grandma Poppy's hutch for the company china and stemware, then polished the silver until it sparkled. While she worked, she worried, wondering what would happen this time to make the evening a flop. In a way, she was almost curious to discover how this particular occasion would be destroyed; at the same time, she was determined to avoid all the most obvious disasters.

Shortly before six, with the house ready and filled with fresh flowers, the table tidily set and all the food ready or cooking, she whipped butter for the bread and corn, made up some fresh poppyseed dressing for the salad, set out a plate of sliced tomatoes and cucumbers, with a few fresh pepper rings added for garnish, and waited, panting as if she'd just finished a marathon race, instead of a marathon cooking session.

Then she suddenly remembered that she had planned to prepare herself as well. In a flurry of activity, she brushed her hair until it gleamed, changed into a fresh white T-shirt with little pink roses in the print—and, of course, her blue jeans—highlighted her eyes with a touch of dark rose shadow and a little mascara, and touched a pink lipstick to her mouth. Then she put on her tiny rose earrings and slipped on her sandals, instead of her indoor house slippers.

At three minutes to six, when her front bell rang, her stomach turned over and she feared she might be ill. *What do I think I'm doing, inviting Joe Vanetti and his family to dinner? I must be nuts!* For one crazy moment, she considered hiding in the back of the house and pretending she wasn't home, but she couldn't imagine anything that might happen this evening that would be worse than having Joe think she'd forgotten him. This *is what you get when you risk being bold*, she warned herself.

Fresh out of options, she pulled her failing courage together. *I'll just pretend I'm the comfortable old maiden aunt*, she thought, and found security in that image. *That's a role I always play well.* Then, feeling much more confident, she went to the door. "Good evening, everyone," she said. Though her stomach was still in turmoil, she was pleased that her voice sounded so calm.

Joe stood on her doorstep looking like the cover of a classy men's magazine. Dressed in simple cotton slacks and a short-sleeved dress shirt, open at the collar, he could easily have been a model in a menswear catalogue. She wondered if heaven had ever created a more attractive male. Just looking at him made her already-queasy tummy turn flip-flops. "Good evening, Angelica," Joe said, and his voice was warmer than the mid-June evening. Then he said something that made no sense at all. "Miss DeForest, I'd like you to meet my children."

"Uh," Angelica hesitated, wondering what she had missed, "I don't understand. I've already met your children."

The mischievous look on Joe's face suggested she was missing something important. "No," he said. "You met Nicholas and Victoria." He laid his hand on his son's shoulder. "Angelica, I'd like you to meet my son, Nick."

"Ah-h-h," Angelica cooed, finally understanding. It delighted her that he had taken their talk at the barbecue to heart. She leaned to take the boy's hand. "I'm so pleased to meet you, Nick."

"And now," Joe said, placing his other hand in the small of his daughter's back, "I'd like you to meet my daughter, Tori."

"Tori?" Angelica asked, taking the girl's hand. "Like Tori Amos?"

The girl erupted in smiles. "Yeah. Uh, I mean, yes, ma'am."

"That's a lovely name," Angelica said, grasping the girl's hand. She caught Joe's questioning expression and flashed him a tell-you-later look, then stepped to one side, waving them all into her entryway. "Please come in, everyone. Dinner's just about ready."

The little family group stepped inside, filling her front room with life and sound. *Old maiden aunt or not*, Angelica thought as she welcomed them, *I think I might just enjoy this evening.* If the look on Joe's face was any indication, things were definitely looking up.

"This looks delicious, Angelica," Joe said, taking the place she indicated at the head of the table. Certainly the larder was full. In the midst of these delightful-looking dishes, a platter full of meat might have seemed superfluous. He didn't add that she looked delicious, too. The little roses on her shirt and in her ears were the perfect complement to her rosy complexion, and he couldn't help admiring the way those jeans accentuated her long, long legs. She seemed friendly, too—more approachable.

He had almost managed to relax at the table when Angelica sat at the opposite end and asked him if he would offer grace, and his discomfiture increased dramatically.

"I, uh . . ." Joe paused. The fact was, despite taking the children to church regularly in order to keep up appearances and maintain their instruction in matters of faith, he hadn't prayed since Roberta's death. He didn't want to now. "I . . ." he began again, but Angelica had closed her eyes and bowed her head, and so had his children. There was no graceful way out of this without either praying, or admitting in front of his children that he no longer prayed. Since he didn't want to do either, he chose the option that he felt would leave him with fewer unpleasant details to clean up later. He bowed his head and said a prayer.

There wasn't much to it, really, just a thanks for good food and a chance to share it with pleasant company. He closed quickly, hoping no one noticed his lack of practice.

Then Angelica, who had served the meal family style, invited everyone to take some of the dish closest and pass to the right. When she picked up a tray of eggplant and offered some to Nicholas, Joe almost spoke up, explaining the boy didn't like eggplant. His intention was cut off when Nick said, "Yes, please," and allowed Angelica to put a slice of the egg-battered vegetable on his plate. Though he wasn't much for eggplant himself, he found Nick's acceptance left him with little option, so he took a slice too, when the tray came to him. Using his fork to cut off a tiny bite, he tasted it and found it surprisingly good.

In fact, the whole meal was delicious. The egg casserole was oozing with cheese and spicy with chilies. The braided loaf was some of the most delicious bread he had ever tasted, and when he asked Angelica where she bought it, he was amazed to learn she had baked it herself, fresh today.

As for the vegetables, Joe stuffed himself on fresh green beans flavored with onions and dill, batter-dipped eggplant—he and Nick each ate four slices—and fresh corn with whipped butter. The green salad was just ordinary salad greens—or was it? There was a variety of leafy greens that Joe couldn't always recognize, and the fresh tomatoes and cukes from Angelica's own garden added delightful flavor and crunch. The extra flavor from the poppyseed dressing meant both his kids, never big on leafy green things, were soon asking for second helpings of salad.

Later, as Nick reached for still more salad, he asked, "What did you call that dressing again?"

"Poppyseed," Angelica answered. "Can I get you some more?"

"Yes, please." Nick held out his plate. "Poppy dressing?" he asked again. "Is that like Grandma Poppy dressing?"

Tori giggled, then said, "No, silly. That's not what it means."

Joe was about to interrupt them—to tell his daughter to behave herself and explain about poppy seeds to his son—when Angelica gave them a gentle smile. "That's right, Nick," she said. "As a matter of fact, this is one of my Grandma Poppy's recipes. Though it's named for the poppy seeds that are in it, I'm sure she wouldn't mind us calling it after her. I may just call it Grandma Poppy dressing from now on, and when I do, I'll think of you."

Nick beamed, Tori quieted without looking the least bit resentful, and Joe wondered if Angelica had studied diplomacy, along with music. It had been more than a year since his children had eaten at the same table without turning it into a war zone. Come to think of it, they'd been sniping at each other pretty good even before Roberta's death. . . .

"Now, if I can just have some help to clear the dishes,

we'll be ready for dessert," Angelica said, drawing his attention back to the table.

"Dessert, too?" he asked, patting his stomach. "I doubt we have room for that."

"You'd be surprised," Angelica said, "but if everyone would prefer, we can just clear the dishes now and save the dessert for later." She turned to his son. "Nick, why don't you stack the plates? Tori, you can put the silverware into that empty serving dish. I'll get the glasses."

Joe couldn't believe it when his children got up and began helping without a single whine. The nightly battle over cleanup had gotten so ugly at his house that he often preferred doing it himself. "How can I help?" he asked, standing.

Angelica flushed—that lovely, rosy blush that made her face seem so alive. "Uh, I hadn't thought . . . Maybe you can carry the leftovers into the kitchen?"

He smiled. If that was a recovery, she'd made it rather quickly. "I'd be happy to," he said, and started picking up serving dishes. When they'd sat down together, he'd have sworn Angelica had cooked enough to feed the Sixth Army. It was surprising how little was left.

The kids stacked plates, silverware, and glasses directly into the dishwasher, following Angelica's directions, and she made quick work of putting away the few leftovers in smaller containers and adding the serving platters and bowls to the dishwasher. "We'll start it after dessert," she said a moment later, then looked around at the expectant family group in her kitchen. "We have an hour or so of sunlight left. Would you like to see my garden?"

"I'd love to," Joe answered, but heard his response drowned in a chorus of excited responses from his kids.

He wondered when they'd become so interested in gardening. *When did you?* he asked himself critically. It occurred to him that something odd was going on here, something he would probably have to think about when he got a few minutes alone. For now, he was content to follow along as Angelica led his son and daughter out her kitchen door and into the backyard.

He'd never been in the backyard of the Lunsford home. He had no idea what he'd been missing. While the front yard was a wide expanse of lawn, with a few leafy trees strategically planted for shade and privacy, the back was a paradise, a large and lovely garden of Eden. Comfortable pathways wound between raised and path-level planting beds, and decorative vegetables mingled with flowering plants—bean vines on six-foot trellises standing side by side with six-foot or taller hollyhocks.

"Wow! This is cool!" Nick turned a full circle, admiring all he saw.

"Gorgeous!" Victoria—*no, Tori; I'm going to have to remember that*—agreed with her brother, using one of her favorite descriptive terms. "Angelica, you must practically live out here to keep up with all of this!"

"Not really," Angelica answered, though Joe could see she was glowing with pride. "It's getting it all started that takes the time. Keeping it up is a matter of an hour or two in the morning, and another hour or two in the evening."

"Every day," Joe added.

Angelica, Tori, and Nick all turned to look at him.

"What I mean is, you have to do it every day to keep it up this nicely."

"Of course," Angelica answered smoothly. She began

walking, taking the children through the garden, showing them what vegetables were ripening now and which would come on later, identifying the different flowering plants and showing the children how the flowers developed from tiny bud to full-blown blossom, then gradually wilted if she didn't pluck them off first.

"Look, here are some green beans ready to pick," she said, and handed Nick a basket she'd picked up on the way out the door. "See where they attach to the vine, Nick? Right here? That's the way. Snap them off just like that. Take any that look fully mature and plop them right into the basket. There you go." Joe shook his head in wonder at the way the boy went readily to work, never questioning the assignment he'd been given or whining about having to help.

"Tori, how'd you like to check out the eggplant?" Angelica asked, and before Joe knew it, both his children were busy working, picking produce from Angelica's garden.

Thus it was that a forty-five-minute walk in Angelica's backyard resulted in a huge basket full of fresh produce: enough green beans for several meals, four large eggplant, a half-dozen green peppers and three red ones, a large batch of fresh spinach and another of Swiss chard, a handful of green onions, a bunch of fresh beets, five small zucchinis and two yellow crookneck squashes, and a stack of assorted fresh salad greens, including some Joe could identify and others he couldn't.

They picked a small batch, ten or so, of Satsuma plums from a tree in one corner of the garden, then finished off the basket with a bouquet of fresh daisies, which Angelica showed Nick how to snip with the clippers, and a second arrangement of a half-dozen rosebuds in a rainbow of hues from pale pink to deep rose to scarlet, yellow to coral to lavender. "There," Angelica said, as she turned them back toward the house. "That ought to keep you in produce for a while."

"Us?" That was the first time Joe rose up to what Angelica was doing. "This is all for us?"

"You didn't think I was going to use this all myself, did you?" Angelica was smiling beatifically.

"But we can't . . . Angelica, we can't take all this."

"Of course you can," she said sweetly. "I have so much more here than I can use." She turned back to the children, leading their way up her back steps into the kitchen. "Tori, you can find some grocery bags in that third drawer down on your left—yes, right there—and Nick, if you'll just step into the back door of the garage, you'll find a small stack of cardboard boxes. I think two ought to do it."

"But Angelica . . ." Joe tried to protest again, but it was clear she wasn't listening. Angelica had had an agenda all along, and she was moving ahead with it, regardless of anything he might say, and with the full cooperation and assistance of his children. He wondered if he'd missed the memo that must have gone around.

"Really, Angelica," he tried again. "It's been a lovely meal, absolutely lovely, but—"

"Thank you," she said, effectively cutting him off as she helped the children organize vegetables and flowers in the two boxes Nick had brought. "I wrote out some recipes before you came." She opened a door off the kitchen and stepped inside, then almost instantly stepped back out with a handful of index cards bound in a rubber band. "If we just add that to the box here, you'll know just what to do with all this food, and how to make that egg casserole, too."

"Thank—" Joe began.

"What's in there?" Nick asked, gesturing at the door Angelica had just entered.

"That's my office," Angelica said, opening the door and turning on the light. "You're welcome to look if you like."

"You have an office?" Tori asked.

"Um-hm." Angelica pushed the door open wider. "That's where I do my work in the mornings. You're welcome to step in and look. Go ahead."

The children stepped into the office and Joe, more curious than he'd imagined, peeked in from the doorway. "What kind of work do you do here?" he asked.

"I'm a medical transcriptionist for the clinic in Holbrook," Angelica answered. "I—"

"Angelica, can we play with your computer?" Nick interrupted her.

Joe started to object, but Angelica murmured, "I don't mind, if you don't."

Then Joe saw an opening he hadn't seen before, a chance for him to speak to Angelica alone while the kids were occupied with something else. "No, I don't mind, as long as you're certain they won't be disturbing anything."

"My work is all put away for the day, so there's really nothing they can disturb," she answered, then stepped inside to help the kids get started with some simple games.

Joe started to speak, but a lump rose in his throat at the mere idea of what he was about to suggest. He cleared his throat and tried again. "Maybe when you get the kids started there, we can talk for a minute? It's nice on the back porch right now, and I noticed there's a porch swing. . . ."

Angelica looked up, her blue eyes wide with surprise, and as cold as January. For a moment, she was the Ice Queen again, and Joe felt a chill run through him. Then she smiled, and it was like dawn breaking over the North Pole, bringing rosy light to everything frozen or icy. "That would be lovely," she said. "Maybe you'd like to pour us some lemonade? There's some all made up in the refrigerator."

"Sounds good," Joe said, and busied himself in the kitchen, finding glasses and pouring lemonade. After a moment, he realized it might take a few minutes for Angelica to get the kids well started. *Good*, he thought. *That will give me a minute to decide if I've lost my mind.* He had been shocked at himself when the idea first occurred to him a few minutes ago, as he watched Angelica working in the garden with his children. Now he was thinking of speaking it aloud. *Well, why not? But it's just as well if I have a minute or two to consider this before she joins me outside*, he thought as he carried the lemonade and two nice glasses out to the porch swing.

"There. You're going now," Angelica said to Nick as he used the mouse like a joystick, fixing leaks in the on-screen pipes before the water could wash them all away. "It will be Tori's turn when the background color changes. Just turn over the mouse then, okay?"

"Gotcha," Nick said as he expertly plugged another leak.

The boy catches on quickly, Angelica thought. *He's really quite bright for a little guy.* But then, both Joe's children had surprised her with their astuteness, their politeness, their almost-grating *adultness*. *He's raising a couple of young Angelicas*, she thought, and wondered if she ought to say something to him about that, though at the moment she was intimidated by the thought of saying much of anything to Joe Vanetti, who through some miracle she couldn't quite fathom, was waiting for her on her back porch swing with a couple of glasses of lemonade.

Good thing I've decided to be bolder, she told herself as she left the children, touched up her hair in a mirror, and started toward the back porch. If she hadn't already committed to being more bold, the very idea of sitting on a porch swing with the hero of her youth would probably have given her apoplexy.

"Hi," she said, smiling as she stepped onto the porch.

"Hi," Joe said, and patted the space beside him on the swing. "Come sit. There's a nice breeze from the hills this evening."

"Umm," she said, making a noncommittal kind of noise. She didn't want him to know she had about all she could do just to keep one foot going in front of the other as she crossed the space that separated her from that porch swing and sitting down next to Joe. Somehow she got there and sat, leaving as much space between them as she could and still be on the same swing. "It is nice out here," she managed to croak out as she joined him.

Joe surveyed the space she had left and she noticed the way his lip quirked up, but he didn't say anything. Instead he handed her a glass of lemonade. "Tell me about your work," he said. "I knew about the music lessons, of course, but I didn't realize you were doing medical work, too."

"Um-hm," she answered, sipping at the lemonade to give her a chance to find her voice. "It isn't really medical work, though, just transcription. After the doctors see a patient at the clinic, they speak their findings about that visit into a tape recorder. At the end of the day, Meryl Banks—she's the receptionist at the clinic—drops the tapes off here on her way home. She leaves them in a drop box at my front door. In fact, I think I heard her drop today's tapes while we were working in the backyard."

"I thought I heard a car," Joe contributed.

"Anyway, I usually get up fairly early and make the rounds in the garden. After awhile, I come in and get ready for the day, then I settle down to transcribing tapes. I have a headset and a foot pedal to move the tape forward or backward, or stop it when I've heard a phrase. I transcribe the notes on each patient separately, entering them all into the computer. At the end of the session, I print them out and put them in a big envelope with the tapes. Then around midday, I drive into Holbrook and drop the notes from the day before at the clinic. Meryl enters each patient's notes into his or her separate file, then puts all the files away until that patient comes in again. That evening, she drops the next day's work in my drop box." She shrugged. "Simple as that. Then I'm back here in time to start my music lessons in the afternoon."

Joe smiled. Angelica thought the expression seemed admiring; she hoped so. "Sounds like a full day," he said. "How'd you get into that? The medical transcribing, I mean."

She sighed and tossed her hair, allowing herself a little freedom. "I suppose it came from years of living with hypochondriacs."

Joe's brows shot up, and she softened her look. "Oh, don't get me wrong, Joe. I loved my mother and my grandmother both dearly, but they became sad, bitter women in their older years. After my father died, my mother was devastated that she hadn't somehow arranged to go with him, and she spent the next twelve years or so trying to die; in fact, she came up with every fatal disease she could imagine and always found all the symptoms of it in herself."

She smiled, hoping to dull the sharp edges of that memory. "We owned a Merck Manual and a P.D.R from the time we moved back here—"

"A what and a what?" Joe asked, obviously lost.

"Sorry. A Merck Manual is a listing of virtually every illness or disease condition known to man, together with all its symptoms and known causes. A P.D.R, is a Physician's Desk Reference. It lists all medications available from various pharmaceutical companies, together with the conditions they're designed to treat, chemical components, possible adverse reactions, and so forth." She smiled, trying to ease her dreary explanations. "Mostly these books are found in doctor's offices, or hospitals and clinics, but my mother arranged to buy copies of both, so she could look up everything on her own. She was always convinced the doctors just weren't listening to her when she described her various disease symptoms. The fact that their tests always came up negative just persuaded her they were all incompetent." She couldn't help chuckling a little, though there wasn't much mirth in it.

"Sounds like it must have been rough, those last few years." Joe's expression was filled with warm sympathy, not the pity she was used to seeing among people who knew her story.

"Sometimes it was," she agreed. "But it taught me everything I ever needed to know about medical terminology. Then after Mother's death, when I had lots of empty hours to fill and Meryl mentioned the clinic had lost its transcriptionist, well . . . it was an easy fit."

"I can see that," Joe said. He put his toe down and pushed, starting the swing rocking. He sipped at his lemonade, creating a quiet pause. After a moment he said, "We've really enjoyed the evening here, Angelica. Thank you for inviting us."

"My pleasure," she answered, glowing under his praise. *If he knew how much . . . But then, perhaps it's better he doesn't.*

"I want to thank you, too, for tipping me about the kids' nicknames," he went on. "If you hadn't said something, I never would have asked them. Then I wouldn't have known that Nicholas prefers to be called Nick, or that Victoria has always wanted to be called Tori. And by the way, who is Tori Amos, anyhow?"

Angelica smiled. "She's a solo artist, a pop singing star," she answered. She saw the look on Joe's face and chuckled. "Don't worry. I wouldn't have known either, except for a piano student of mine who wanted to play a Tori Amos piece. She brought me the music, but it was way too complex for her. From the looks of it, I'd say Tori Amos must be quite a pianist, too."

"I'd have had no idea," Joe said.

"If it hadn't been for that student, I never would have

known. I didn't even keep up with pop music when I was that age, I'm afraid."

Joe nodded. "I remember. I mean, I remember that you were always into the more classical kinds of music." He gave her an apologetic smile that suggested to Angelica that he remembered much more than she had ever imagined. "By the way, are you ready to be called Angie? I mean, now that my kids are taking nicknames . . ."

"Oh, no. I don't feel like an Angie anymore," Angelica answered. "The idea of having a nickname isn't so bad. But it's been years since I felt like an Angie." She smiled. "I may have to keep working on that one."

"It just seemed fair," Joe said, but Angelica discouraged him with a wag of her head. For a moment they rocked slowly and silently, sipping at their drinks. Then Joe said, "Thanks so much for the vegetables and the recipes and everything. I didn't intend to raid your garden when we came over."

"It was hardly a raid. As I recall, I had to insist that you take it all."

"You will at least let me pay you for it, won't you?" Joe reached for his wallet.

"Nonsense. And I mean that."

But Joe took out his wallet anyway. "How much do you think—?"

"Joe Vanetti, don't you dare touch that wallet!"

Her vehemence surprised even herself. When Joe looked up with a half-frightened, half-admiring expression, she gently added, "How can I be neighborly if you insist on paying for the produce? Besides, I always grow more than I can use. It will be a relief to have someone using the extra—especially if you like the zucchini. By August, I'll have enough for any ten families."

"Okay, then," Joe said, putting his wallet away. "Then maybe you'll let me pay you to cook for us?"

Angelica felt her stomach sink. *Is that why he wanted to talk to me alone?* "Cook for you?" she asked. "You mean, regularly?" She could almost picture herself as an adopted maiden aunt, or maybe even a friend of the family, but not as a cook. No, she definitely didn't want to picture herself as a paid domestic in that family's home.

Joe lit up. "Would you consider it? I've never seen my kids eat my cooking the way they ate here tonight. You'd think I'd been deliberately starving the poor hungry waifs."

"Joe, I don't know how to say this, but I really can't picture myself as a cook." Angelica was trying not to be hurt that that's what he had seen in her.

"I know it's not what you normally do, and you're already quite busy with the transcribing and the music lessons and the garden and whatnot, but it isn't just the cooking. There's so much—"

"Please stop." Angelica cringed, willing down the burning in her eyes. *I don't want to hear any more about how you think of me. It hurts too much.* "Please, Joe."

He must have seen the look on her face. "Angelica, I didn't mean—"

"It's okay," she said. "Just don't tell me how much I remind you of Hazel, the maid on the old TV show." She tried to smile at her wry joke, but the tear trickling down her cheek was spoiling the effect.

"Angelica, that's not what I was trying to say—"

But she was already standing. "Thanks so much for coming tonight, Joe. It was good to visit with Tori and Nick. I'll see Tori Wednesday afternoon at her violin lesson. Now if you will excuse me . . ."

Joe stood, too. "Angelica—"

"If you will please excuse me," she repeated.

"Angelica. I—" Then he did something that neither of them expected. He stepped close, took her by the shoulders, and kissed her firmly on the lips.

For a moment the world spun around her, a daze of confusion. Then, as Joe drew away, Angelica surfaced into a bright new world—a world in which Joe Vanetti could find someone like her attractive enough to kiss.

"I . . . I apologize. I shouldn't have done that," Joe was saying, though his voice seemed to be coming from somewhere far away. "I just want you to know that I don't think of you as a maid. That's all." He touched her shoulder. "Angelica? Angelica, are you all right?"

It took a moment for her to realize that someone had asked her a question and that somehow, she was expected to respond. She managed, slowly, to nod her head.

"Good," he said. "Angelica, I really am sorry. I don't quite know what came over . . . I guess I'd better be going now." He started for the back door.

Just as he entered it, Angelica found her voice. "Joe?"

He turned, a hangdog expression on his handsome features. "Yes?"

"I'll see you Wednesday, for Tori's lesson."

He nodded. "Wednesday," he said, and the single word rang with promise.

Chapter Four

What was I thinking? Joe asked himself that Tuesday as he struggled to listen to all the design and operating specifications for the power plant that was his new responsibility. *Was I thinking at all? Did I really kiss Angelica DeForest—Miss DeForestation of Rainbow Rock High School?*

He wasn't sure where that impulse had come from, but he was relatively certain the kiss had been real. He'd been tasting it all night in his dreams. He hadn't kissed a woman in the more than fourteen months since his wife's death. In fact, unless sympathy hugs from family and friends could be counted—and Joe didn't think they could—he hadn't so much as held a woman in all that time.

That hadn't kept him from holding Angelica. Even now, when he was supposed to be listening to a rundown on the boiler tolerances at the plant, he could still feel her slender shoulders going rigid, then softening beneath his palms. Even now, when he was supposed to be memorizing the procedure for initiating an emergency shutdown, he could still smell the clean, slightly floral scent of her hair, still feel the warm, moist caress of her lips.

I'm losing it, that's all. I'm just losing it, he recited like a mental litany as the boiler room manager showed him where emergency procedures were posted. He gave the man a vacant half-smile in response to something he'd said, then wondered if perhaps the fellow had asked a question and he should have had an answer ready.

So why did I kiss Angelica? he asked himself as he looked out over the wetlands created by the lake's formation. Then as the grounds manager began a discussion of the company's policies to encourage waterbird habitat, he answered his own question: *It doesn't matter why I did it. I'm glad I did.* As much as the whole situation confused him, he could hardly wait until he could drive Tori to her lesson on Wednesday afternoon. That would give him an excuse to see Angelica again.

Mrs. Hodge, Nolan Steckle, Judy Rossiter—Angelica thumbed through the printouts she'd just completed before adding them to the file. Several of the "usual suspects" had turned up at the doctor's office in yesterday's visits, as well as a few who hadn't been there in a while, and one or two names she didn't recall having seen before. Since she'd begun this job she'd often reflected that it was just as well she wasn't very sociable. Knowing as much as she did about people's private medical problems might have created a moral dilemma, were she inclined to gossip.

Today was one of the first times in a long time that

she'd wished she'd had someone around to gossip with. In fact, she went to the phone several times, thinking of calling her cousin, Heidi.

But what would I tell her? she reflected each time she set the phone back in its cradle. *That Joe Vanetti came to dinner at my house? That he brought his children to eat a meatless meal, then asked me to cook for him? That he kissed me before he left?* Perhaps that was why she seemed unable to go through with the phone call. In the eighteen hours or so since Joe's kiss, it had been about all Angelica could do to get herself to believe it. She couldn't have expected Heidi, or anyone else, to believe it as well.

Joe Vanetti kissed me, she thought as she loaded the things she needed to take back to the clinic in Holbrook. *Joe kissed me!* Though she felt fairly certain he'd done it largely to help him explain something he was finding it difficult to put into words, the fact remained that he'd done it. The touch of his hands, the brush of his lips, the nearness and the heat of him had all been real, and more vivid than any dream she'd ever had. *Joe Vanetti kissed me*, she thought again as she slipped into a T-shirt, jeans, and sandals, and popped behind the wheel of her car.

On the spur of the moment, she decided something as impetuous as Joe's kiss deserved a celebration in kind. She'd have lunch today at the Kachina Café, a sort of treat to reward herself for this new approach to boldness that had already brought such new and unexpected delights into her life. *Well, okay, delights and complications*, she added, recognizing that that one gentle kiss, as minor as it probably was in the life of a man like Joe, was going to make it tougher than she'd ever imagined to see him again when he brought his daughter over to-morrow afternoon.

It's worth it, she concluded with a grin as she turned her car toward the freeway. *It's worth any complications that may arise.* That decided, it occurred to her that she might take advantage of the opportunity to do a little shopping while she was in Holbrook. She thought she could use a nice summer shirt and another pair, maybe two, of blue jeans.

2:27. That's the slowest clock in America. Joe watched the hands tick away the dragging seconds, wondering vaguely why his sense of time was so distorted. He'd figured out the schedule with his supervisors before he'd even started working here, so he wasn't worried about taking time away to take Tori (he felt pleased that he'd remembered) to her lesson. He was salaried, after all, and putting in plenty of hours as it was.

So if the schedule isn't worrying me, what is? Clearly, there was something going on. He knew worry when he felt it, and the way his body was knotted up all over was a clear indication if he'd ever felt one. He set down the tools he'd been using to take the temperature of water samples from the boiler exit pipes, and concentrated on taking three deep breaths, then resumed measuring again. *Okay, it's not the schedule*, he thought, running through a potential checklist. *And it's not Vic . . . it's not Tori. She seems really excited about this lesson. Angelica said . . . Whoa!*

The moment he'd thought Angelica's name, the un-comfortable tightening in his gut told him he'd found the source of his unease. *Admit it, Vanetti*, he thought with a sigh. *The woman has you tied up in knots.*

There'd have been little point in trying to deny it. He'd been a basket case ever since Monday evening when he'd tried to hire Angelica as his cook, then kissed her as a form of apology. If he'd had any idea of how he, himself, would react to that kiss, he'd have thought twice before allowing it to happen. Oh, no doubt it had been wonderful, so wonderful he'd thought—or dreamed—of little else for two days. But it had been so long since he'd held a woman. Was it Angelica who had thrilled him? Or just the fact that he'd finally kissed a woman again? And was it fair to Angelica that he'd kiss her for so little cause—no cause at all, really—when all he really wanted, or needed, was the opportunity to feel once more like a healthy, red-blooded man with an attractive woman in his arms?

So what I'm afraid of, he summed up, letting the water sample in his leather gloves grow cold, *is seeing her again.*

He shivered, imagining himself being greeted at the door by the Ice Queen in full regalia, her cool blue stare pinning him to the wall like an insect on a scientist's corkboard. Surely a cool, refined woman like Angelica . . .

He paused, unable to finish that thought, for it wasn't the cool, refined Ice Queen whose image rose up in his mind. It was the passionate artist he remembered just now, the fiercely intense woman with the delicate fingers and the fire in her eyes who had stroked that viola with such ardor. The image made his throat tighten and his mouth go dry. Was it Angelica's coldness he feared? Or was it the heat she engendered in him?

Whoa! That thought hit too close to the truth. *Admit it, Vanetti. Angelica gets to you in ways you're just not ready for.* He drew back from that realization with a start, finding it difficult to imagine that it was really Angelica DeForest—the Miss DeForestation of his youth—who had inspired such a heated response.

Almost three-thirty. He—no, they—will be here any minute. Angelica studied her mirrored image critically, wondering if she might have overdone it. She was wearing her new blue jeans, and a form-fitting T-shirt in rich navy blue. She'd bought a new pair of sandals, and she'd painted her toenails, as well as her fingernails, in vivid pink. She wore the pink rosebud earrings, and she'd taken great care with her makeup and brushed her hair till it glistened like spun honey. *The key is to be nonchalant about this*, she told herself firmly, *as if I always dress this way when I give a lesson.* Then she snorted at her own foolishness. *No man in his right mind is going to believe that one!*

Well, okay then, she said, taking another tack. *Let him figure out that I'm dressing for him. Let him guess that he attracts me, that I wouldn't mind doing a little attracting myself.* She quailed at the thought. If she put herself forward in that way, and it turned out he was really only interested in having someone to cook for his children . . . *Well, that's the risk one takes, isn't it?* she told herself, lifting her chin in a brave, or defiant, gesture. Boldness had its downside, but it had to be better than not trying.

The ringing doorbell caused a moment's panic, and a threatened change of heart. But Angelica looked her reflection in the eye, squared her shoulders, and went to the door. Whatever the next hour might bring, it would almost be worth it, just to see Joe Vanetti again.

* * *

"Lovely. Just lovely. So how do you do with the scales in the minor keys?"

Joe watched in fascination as Angelica led his daughter through the minor scales. The Ice Queen he had feared had failed to materialize. Instead he'd been greeted by the consummate artist, the woman of depth and passion, who had flashed her radiant eyes at him with such tantalizing smiles that he'd been tempted to kiss her again, just to see if she tasted as good as he remembered.

You're losing it, Joe, he told himself firmly. *This is Angelica DeForest we're talking about. Make a move and she'll freeze you solid with a glance.* But he was lying to himself and he knew it. It wasn't Angelica's coolness he feared. From the moment he'd seen her again, the instant, heated reaction he had was telling him otherwise.

Since lying to himself wasn't working, he decided to try reasoning. As he watched Angelica move with such appealing grace, he told himself firmly that it did him no good to want what he could not have. Then another thought beckoned. *But what if . . .*

Joe cut off the thought, shot through with a sudden, piercing stab of disloyalty. Since the day he'd first seen Roberta, he'd never so much as touched another woman. He'd barely even looked at one. He and Roberta had been the perfect pairing—practically everyone said so— and their marriage had been a haven from the pressures and problems of the world, a safe harbor where they both could rest, assured of perfect trust and fidelity. Didn't he still owe her that faith? After all, it wasn't her idea to die on the freeway in a tangle of metal and pain.

Joe closed his eyes against the images that assailed him, images he'd been choking back since the uniformed officers had come to his door with the news of Roberta's death.

"Joe, are you all right?" The hand that warmed his shoulder brought him back from the world of nightmares into the brilliant light of Angelica's gaze. Her face was rosy with blushing and she drew her hand away, then stammered in apology as he stared at her. "I'm sorry if I bothered . . . You seemed so . . ."

"It's all right," he said, taking her hand. "I'm okay. Sorry if I troubled you."

She offered an unsteady smile, then went back to working with his daughter, while Joe chided himself for letting his memories invade the present moment. *But one thing's clear*, he told himself as he watched Angelica work. *I'm really not ready to feel what I'm feeling here. What I need is a little distance from the lovely Miss DeForest—even if that's not what I think I want.*

The lesson was nearly over, and Angelica listened with only half an ear as Tori bowed her way through the simple Béla Bartók piece. Though she watched the daughter, her mind was focused on the father. He'd frightened her in that tense moment when he'd closed his eyes and his face had contorted in pain. She'd glanced at him frequently since then, assuring herself he was well.

Some inner instinct, born perhaps from her years of patient caregiving, told her Joe's pain wasn't physical. That frightened her even more. Whatever had brought that agony to his face still rested in his heart, waiting to sabotage him in any vulnerable moment, and it was only in his vulnerable moments that she stood a chance of reaching high enough to touch Joe's pedestal.

"That's fine, just fine," she said as Tori finished the Bartók. "Some of the best sight-reading I've seen. Work on that piece for next week, and start the Beethoven as well."

"Okay," Tori agreed. She took the violin down from her shoulder, and Angelica handed her the violin case that had rested beneath her piano during the lesson.

"How are you doing with the vegetables I sent home?" Angelica asked as Victoria cared for her violin, hoping to include Joe in the conversation.

"Fine," Tori answered. "Dad cooked some spinach for dinner last night, and I helped him stir-fry some squash and green onions."

"Great!" Angelica answered. Then turning to Joe, "You can add the spinach to a salad, too. Have you used the poppyseed dressing I sent?"

When Joe didn't answer immediately, Tori spoke. "Not yet," she said, "but I think I'll make a salad for dinner tonight—if that's okay with you, Dad."

"Yeah. Yeah, that'll be fine." The words seemed to be torn from Joe, who never quite met Angelica's gaze.

A chill went down her spine. Whatever had happened in those awkward moments still haunted Joe Vanetti, still tightened his throat and robbed his eyes of their sparkle. The evidence of his pain was so tangible that it very nearly stole Angelica's resolve. If she had not sworn herself to boldness, she'd have shrunken back into the wallpaper she came out of, simply disappearing from sight.

But she had sworn it, hadn't she? She lifted her chin, and spoke the words she had so carefully rehearsed. "I'm guessing you'll run out of vegetables by the weekend. Would you like to come to dinner again on Monday?"

"I don't think . . . We can't . . ." Joe stood, and a look something like panic swept across his features. "I'm sorry. I really need to go," he said, starting for the front door.

"Da-ad . . ." Tori was watching him with a look of abject horror. "Angelica's trying to be *nice* to us."

Angelica saw the indecision warring in Joe's eyes, then he sighed and a look she could only describe as resignation took its place. "All right," he said, though his look suggested that eating dinner with Angelica was about as welcome as facing a firing squad. "We'll be happy to have dinner here on Monday. Thank you."

"Is six still good?" Angelica asked, though her own throat had now tightened painfully.

"Six it is," Joe said. "Come on, Tori. Let's go."

Angelica watched him rush for his car. The poor man was practically sprinting. She didn't know what had happened here, couldn't imagine what awful thing she might have done, but whatever it was had Joe Vanetti fleeing as if chased by an armed mob.

As she stood in the window, watching him flee, Angelica resolved to make Monday evening as pleasant as possible. After that, if Joe wasn't any happier than this about being in her presence . . . *Well, at least I'll know I gave it my best shot*, she told herself, though she took little comfort in the thought.

An agonizing five days had passed since his last visit to Angelica's. Except for nodding politely at church, Joe hadn't seen or spoken to her, but she'd haunted his thoughts, creating a gentle possession he hadn't known since his early days with Roberta. Now, as he herded his children through the process of getting ready for dinner in her home, he wondered what enchantment Angelica owned to turn his thoughts so frequently in her direction, or to bring him into her presence again, even when he'd sworn to keep his distance.

The tension between what he claimed he needed and what he knew he wanted was exhausting him, wearing thin his patience and causing him to growl or snap frequently at his children. They had noticed, and had begun to hang back even more than before, treating him with a diffidence that almost broke his heart. He didn't like the person he was becoming, and that too he blamed on Angelica. Then, cursing himself for his unfairness, he fell back on guilty remonstrations, and resented her even more for causing him to feel guilty as well as unfair.

Something's gotta give, he warned himself as he drove toward her home, tension roiling his gut. For the life of him, he couldn't figure out what it was going to be.

"Ouch!" Angelica dropped the knife that had grazed the edge of her middle finger, not quite breaking the skin. *That was a close one*, she thought as she popped the offended finger into her mouth.

It's the tension, she admitted uneasily. *This is even worse than last week.* Many times during the past five days she had very nearly called the whole thing off, certain Joe didn't want to be here and fearful of how she'd behave under the sting of his disquiet. *The tension is eating my brain.* She gave the knife a disgusted huff and tossed it into the sink, then surveyed the results of two days' work.

It had taken only minutes after Joe and his children

had left the week before for her to discover she had never served the dessert she'd so carefully prepared. This week she'd make sure to bring the dessert out before she allowed a visit into the garden, or anything else, to keep her from serving the fresh strawberry glaze pies she had labored over. *If the way to a man's heart is through his stomach . . .*

She stopped herself, heartsick and on the verge of tears. Was she really so desperate that she thought a strawberry pie would make Joe want to be with her when he clearly wanted to be almost anywhere else?

This has got to stop. Her face set in determination, she went to the phone and punched in the number she had memorized, after all the times she'd looked it up during the week. She'd simply call Joe and tell him she was sorry, but something had come up and she couldn't make their dinner appointment. That would give them both an easy out, and they'd never have to face each other. She'd never have to see that trapped animal look that had come over him when his daughter had backed him into accepting her invitation, and she'd never have to hear the excuses he would already have prepared for why they couldn't ever come here again, maybe even why he'd prefer to drive his daughter to Flagstaff for her future violin lessons.

The phone rang ten times before Angelica gave up, then glanced at the clock and realized Joe was probably already on his way. By the time the doorbell rang seconds later, she knew it was too late to change her mind. *I'll just have to make the best of it*, she told herself, but she walked toward the door like a condemned soul goes to the gallows. Pasting on her jovial maiden aunt expression, she opened the door.

*   *   *

She's beautiful, Joe thought as Angelica greeted them. *So beautiful.* He had spent these past days hardening his heart against the appeal of this lovely woman, telling himself it was only his loneliness, only his long months without a woman's touch that had made her look so good to him in the first place. During the past five near-sleepless nights, he had conjured as many images as he could recall of the Ice Queen of his youth, remembering times when she'd tripped and fallen, or had run for the bathrooms covered in ketchup and mustard, fortifying himself with layers of solid ice packed tightly around his heart. All of those images evaporated now as he faced the simple reality of Angelica, looking every bit as angelic as her name. In that moment, the protective ice layers melted into vapor, and Joe knew what had to give.

"Hello," he said, leaning to brush her cheek with his lips. "Thank you so much for having us again."

"Y . . . you're welcome," the angel before him said, her sky-blue eyes wide with surprise, and he knew she'd been expecting the coldness or anger that everyone around him had been reaping this past week.

He glanced at his children, both of whom stared at him in openmouthed astonishment, and knew he had much to atone for. "Dinner smells fantastic," he declared with an expansive gesture. "What're we having?"

"Spinach quiche," Angelica responded, still looking a bit shell-shocked. "And lots of vegetables."

"Of course," Joe answered. "Sounds delicious. Come on, kids. Let's eat." He led the way to the table and took the same place he'd had the week before. Then, before he could let go of his good-guy resolve, he even volunteered to offer grace on their meal.

As he said the simple prayer, he realize
thing even deeper, even more withheld than ̣
about Angelica, had melted within him. For the firṣ ̣
in nearly fifteen months, he felt that Someone on the
other end was listening.

It had been a near-perfect evening, or so Angelica decided as she turned on the dishwasher and finished the
small batch of hand-washing. Joe had raved about the
spinach quiche and even Nick, though he'd expressed
doubts about eating "spinach pie," had wolfed down seconds, then thirds. The salad, complete with Grandpa
Poppy dressing, had been as big a hit this week as last,
and the four vegetable dishes had vanished as if she really was feeding the Sixth Army. They kids had enjoyed
her fresh-baked raisin bread so much that she'd sent a
second loaf home with Tori, along with a batch of recipes and another huge box of garden produce. Then
everyone had raved about the fresh strawberry pies.

Though Joe had been charming—at least as appealing
as he'd ever been in his youth—he'd made a point of
avoiding any of those moments alone with her on the
porch. *And I'd been hoping he'd kiss me again*, Angelica
realized as she turned off the kitchen lights and prepared
for sleep. Even with the odd unease she'd sensed in Joe
during this past week, some part of her had reached beyond reason to hope for another small show of intimacy,
another hint that he might think of her as more than a
convenience, or even a friend.

That kiss on the cheek was something of a surprise,
though, wasn't it? she asked herself as she cleaned her
face and brushed her teeth. She rinsed and put away her
toothbrush, then paused, looking her reflection in the eye

and trying to add up the clues. They didn't make sense.

He'd been so uneasy with her on Wednesday that she'd feared he'd never want to return, then he'd avoided speaking to her for the five days in between. Yet this evening he'd greeted her at the door as if they were long-lost pals. He'd been pleasant and personable throughout dinner, dessert, and another productive tour of her garden, and he'd thanked her profusely as he'd left, carrying another batch of homegrown vegetables with him. Angelica grimaced at herself and turned away from the mirror. If there was a pattern to be discerned here, she had no clue what it was.

But it certainly feels good to know he's not as unhappy here as he was last week. As she settled down to sleep, she took comfort in that thought.

At home in his own bed, Joe was running the same tally, and it didn't add up to him, either. All he knew for sure was, the way he'd been behaving all week wasn't Angelica's fault, or his children's, and it simply wasn't fair to take his frustrations out on them. So he'd greeted Angelica as he would a sister, or a pal, and had simply avoided being alone with her.

It worked, too, he thought, practically purring with satisfaction. *Maybe that's the key. I don't have to avoid Angelica completely. I can take my daughter to her lessons and even eat dinner with Angelica if she invites me. Maybe I can even return the favor and take her out to eat once in a while. Sure, I'd do that with anyone else who invited us over, wouldn't I? I just need to make sure we're always thoroughly chaperoned, with Vic . . . with Tori and Nick close by.*

He relaxed, pleased with himself. After all, it wasn't

as if they were dating. He'd already worked his way through that one. They were old friends—well, sort of—who were enjoying the chance to get reacquainted after long years apart. He could spend time around her and maybe even chat a little, get to know her some, and as long as they were always in the company of his children, or others, he'd never need to worry about betraying Roberta. The attraction he felt could remain his own little secret.

Contented, Joe drifted into sleep, images of a honeyblond angel crowding his thoughts, never once admitting that maybe he was lying to himself about the size of his "little secret" or the ease of keeping it to himself.

Tori's lesson went splendidly. Angelica couldn't have been happier with her progress. She had mastered the Bartók—had even committed it to memory!—and needed only a little more work to have the Beethoven down as well. In Victoria Vanetti, Angelica found a combination of natural musical gifts and willingness to work that almost guaranteed success. There was no telling how far the child would wish to pursue her talent, but Angelica felt certain that if she wanted a professional performing career, even that would be within her reach.

"She's doing beautifully," she told Joe as the girl finished her lesson and put away her instrument. "Tori has all the makings of a very fine musician."

Joe's paternal pride glowed in his eyes. "Others have told me she's talented, but I've never been able to tell one way or the other, since I know so little about music myself. I want to thank you again for taking her as a student."

"I won't be able to take her far, given the rate she's

progressing. Another year or so, and she'll need a specialist, someone who knows the violin better than I."

"That soon?"

"If she keeps up this way."

"I won't go this fast once school starts," Tori interrupted, speaking for herself. "I get bored with nothing to do in the summer, so I sometimes practice two or three hours a day. I can't do that once classes are back in session."

"True, that could slow things down," Angelica agreed. "We'll just see how you do, okay?"

Tori smiled—a smile that struck Joe as so much simpler and more natural than most of those he'd seen in recent months. He remembered the other purpose he'd had in mind for today.

"Anyway, as I said, I want to thank you for taking her as a student, and for having us over for dinner, twice now, and for all the delicious produce you've sent home with us both weeks." He grinned, then before Angelica could demur, he quickly added, "The kids and I would like to invite you to eat out with us this Friday after I get off work. It won't be anything fancy. Nick likes the barbecue place here in town. I checked their menu and they have some meatless options for those who don't eat barbecue—"

"That's okay. I've been meatless for a while now. The barbecue sounds good," Angelica interjected.

"You'll join us then?"

"I'd love to." Her smile lit the room.

"Then we'll see you Friday," he said. "We'll pick you up around six?"

"That'll be fine."

Joe left the Lunsford home feeling good about the

compromise he'd come to. He and Angelica weren't dating as long as the kids were with then, and the presence of his children would keep him from acting on any more unpredictable impulses. It was the perfect solution. He felt pleased with himself—downright smug, in fact. Everything was working out beautifully.

Chapter Five

"Pass the salt, please," Nick asked.

"Here you go." Angelica passed along the salt and pepper shakers.

They had ordered four of the house specials, and were all busy enjoying their meal. Joe couldn't help noticing his kids seemed more relaxed than they had in some time. Even Angelica seemed to relish the delicious slow-roasted barbecue.

"So tell me, Nick," she asked as she set down her fork. "You're going to be in third grade this year, right?"

"Yes, ma'am." Nick had to swallow fast in order to answer.

"And you were on a soccer team before you moved out here?"

"Yeah," Nick said. "I mean, yes ma'am, but Dad says there isn't a soccer league for kids my age out here."

"No, not that I know of," Angelica said. "I know they play intramural soccer at the junior high."

"That's *years* away." Nick pouted.

"The lack of soccer is still a point of contention," Joe mumbled, and Angelica nodded understanding.

"You know, we may not have an organized league," she said, "but I'll bet there are a lot of other kids who'd like to get together to learn how to play, if you wanted to show them."

"You think?" Joe felt touched by the way Nick brightened.

"Um-hm, I think so." Angelica grinned. "What position do you usually play?"

"I'm a forward," Nick answered, and launched into a lively description of games he'd played in and goals he'd scored.

Angelica nodded sagely. "You might start with your cousin Danny," she said. "I'm sure he'd get a kick out of playing soccer, especially this summer when there's not much to do. Then I'll bet he's got some buddies who'd like to play. Lydia and Tori might want to play, too. You could probably get a pretty good pickup game going."

"That sounds good," Nick said. "Where do you think we could play?"

"Maybe at the soccer fields at the junior high? It should be an easy bike ride from your house, or from your Aunt Cretia's."

"You're right." He turned to his sister. "What d'ya think, Victoria—I mean, Tori? You wanta help me get some kids together for a soccer game?"

"What would we do for a net at the goal?" Tori asked, looking toward Angelica.

"You might have to play without nets to begin with."

"We could just count it as a goal if it went between the stripes," Nick said, and Tori nodded. Soon the children were busy planning between bites, deciding when and how they'd organize their first game in the unofficial Rainbow Rock Youth Soccer League.

Joe watched in amusement, then amazement, as his children became more animated than he'd seen them in some time. They were acting like children for the first time in many months, and Angelica was the key. It was she who had helped them start this, and she was keeping them going now, adding a helpful idea now and then when the kids became frustrated.

Already, he reflected with some surprise, she had been a blessing in their lives. Even he had been changed. Since praying at her dinner table earlier this week, he had begun to pray with his children again. Then last night, before dropping exhausted into bed, he'd offered the first personal prayer he'd said in fifteen months. Now his children, who had been sullen, silent watchers in his home since he'd announced the move to Arizona, were finding reasons to like being here. It was a blessing to be able to watch them blossom and grow again, like young plants too long neglected, now thriving under a gardener's tender care—and Angelica was the gardener. He listened as Nick and Tori laughed at something Angelica had shared with them, and felt another layer of the protective ice around his heart begin to melt, leaving his heart exposed and vulnerable.

By the time everyone had finished eating, he was beginning to feel that mildly panicky sensation that suggested he was falling too far under Angelica's spell. *She's supposed to be an Ice Queen*, he reflected wryly, *not a fairy queen capable of charming my heart out of my chest. I need to get some control here.*

Nick announced, "I'm ready for dessert, Dad."

"I want the cheesecake this time," Tori said.

"I have a better idea." Joe spoke quickly, hoping to do a quick detour and maneuver them all out of such close quarters. "Let's walk down the street toward the park. There's an ice cream parlor on the corner. We can get cones and eat them there. What d'ya think?"

"Cool," Tori said.

"Yeah, cool," Nick agreed.

Angelica lit the room with a smile like the sun rising over the painted desert. *I should take that as a simple yes*, Joe thought, but he couldn't help noticing the way his heart picked up speed when she smiled at him. *Nothing simple about that . . .*

He paid their check and they began a slow stroll down the walk. It wasn't long before they had their cones— Angelica had asked for a single scoop of French vanilla—and the kids had scattered in the park. That was when Joe realized his mistake. He'd been looking to get some distance, to reduce the impact of the intimate surroundings in the small restaurant. Now he sat on a park bench with Angelica by his side, the two of them alone in the shadows of a near-perfect evening, his homegrown chaperones at a distance. The sun was setting behind the San Francisco peaks, near Flagstaff, its brilliant red-orange glow turning Angelica's honeyed hair to flame, and all he wanted was to get his hands into that hair.

I'm in real trouble, he thought without a single sign of worry, suddenly not caring if this kind of trouble came to claim him. *But I do have to keep my wits about me. I'd only frighten Angelica if I touched her hair the way I want to*, and so he kept his hands to himself. He watched Angelica as she relished her French vanilla, her perfect blue eyes flashing at him in mixed innocence and invitation. *I wonder if she has a clue what she's doing to me,* he thought.

She paused between licks. "I was just thinking about the first time I ever met you," she said, and Joe sputtered to keep from choking on his ice cream.

"You remember that?" he asked.

"Um-hm." Another lick. "It was my first day of school at Rainbow Rock Junior High School. My father had died during the year before, and my mother moved us out to live with Grandma Poppy just before the school year began. I was in seventh grade, the new girl in school, scared of everybody, and you were the eighth-grade King of the Mountain. I remember how you stood in front of the school explaining registration procedures to all the younger kids." She licked her ice cream again.

"I wouldn't have guessed you'd remember something like that," he said, at a loss to think of anything else.

"Of course I did," she said, and licked the ice cream again. "You were like that just now in the restaurant, and again at the ice cream parlor—organizing everyone, taking charge. It was one of the things I always—" She paused. "—one of the things I always admired about you." She flushed that lovely rosy color and ducked her head, taking refuge in licking her ice cream.

Angelica admired me? The thought was a paradigm shift as momentous as the discovery that the earth was round. The idea that the perfect, untouchable Angelica DeForest had admired him was almost more than he could accept. *It was tough for her to admit that, too*, he realized, watching the richness of her blush. *I need to say something*. "I remember that day," he said, finishing his cone and setting the paper napkin aside.

"You do?"

He nodded. "Um-hm. It was the first time any of us had ever seen you, so we were all curious about the new girl," he explained, not adding that her uncommon beauty had added to his own interest. "You were wearing a blue tartan plaid with red and yellow stripes in it. It was sort of a jumper, with a white turtleneck. And you had on white socks with lace around the tops."

"Yes," Angelica said, her own face alight with wonder, and Joe wondered if the earth had just turned round for her as well. "You remember the socks?"

"I'd never seen anyone wear socks with lace like that, except on TV. My sister never wore socks like that. No one I knew did."

"So you remembered the socks," Angelica said, and there was a wry edge to her comment.

"And the tartan plaid jumper," he added. Then he took a deep breath. "Mostly I think I remembered your hair. It was such a pretty blond color. It looked so—" This time he paused, then getting up his courage, added, "—so touchable."

"Oh." Angelica flushed again, and he knew what she must be thinking, since his own thoughts had so recently dealt with the same shifting paradigm.

Then he looked around and noticed that somehow, subtly, he had moved toward her, or she toward him, or both toward one another. They sat very close together now, close enough that if he had leaned just a little— Joe cut off that thought before he could admit what he'd been thinking, but the image of her eyes drifting closed as her lips opened under his was already planted firmly in his mind, the physical memory of their first kiss already searing his mouth.

He jumped to his feet, grabbing the paper napkin he'd set down a moment before. "Are you finished with that ice cream?" he asked. "I'll take the paper to the trash if you're done. Then I think it's time to call the kids."

"Okay," she said, handing him her paper napkin. He didn't understand why she looked so crestfallen.

"Good night. Thanks again for dinner." Angelica shut the car door behind her as she started up the walk. Joe waited until she had let herself in the front door, then pulled away from her curb as she waved good-bye. *Well,* she told of herself as the car disappeared at the end of the block, *that was certainly* . . . She hunted for a word. She couldn't find one. Throughout the past couple of weeks since Joe Vanetti had returned to town, she had wondered what might happen if they spent an evening together. Now she knew, only she wasn't sure what it was she knew.

She had subjugated her image of her mother and Grandpa Poppy both lecturing that a woman must *never* be forward with a man, and had pulled together all her flagging courage and newfound boldness to share her first memories of Joe, and to admit she had admired him. That was such a brave new world for her that she thought she'd have died on the spot if Joe had made fun of her. Instead he'd shared a memory of her socks—her *socks,* for heaven's sake!—and while she was delighted that he had remembered her, she couldn't help wondering if it was the oddity of lace socks that he'd remembered, not her at all.

But then there had been that incongruous moment when he'd commented on her hair and had leaned toward her. . . . For a breathless moment, she'd been sure he was going to kiss her, and she'd wanted that kiss more than she had imagined, more than she knew she could, almost more than she wanted her own breath.

Well, at least I've invited him for dinner again on Monday, she told herself as she locked the front door behind her and readied herself for sleep. *At least I have him coming back for more.* She didn't want to think too much about more what, lest he be filled with memories of lacy white socks.

It was Monday evening. Grace had been said and the food had been served, and Tori and Nick were talking about their first soccer game, which they'd managed to pull together that Saturday afternoon. They'd played two teams against each other, both short a couple of players, and they'd had to do it without nets at the goal boxes and with no official timekeeper. Still they'd had a great time and they eagerly awaited the next game, scheduled for Wednesday after Tori's lesson.

"I think Danny can find a couple more big guys," Nick was saying. Joe listened approvingly as he took yet another bite of the baked spiced eggplant.

"Lydia has some girlfriends who might want to join us, too," Tori added, "including some younger kids more my age."

"That'll be neat," Nick said. "That way you can meet more kids in your class before school starts."

"Yeah. I'm looking forward to that."

Joe beamed at them both, pleased that his kids were doing so well after only a few weeks in their new home, and grateful to Angelica for all she'd done to make it possible.

"I never thought we'd settle in this quickly," Tori was saying. Joe noticed she'd finished a second helping of the Brussels sprouts. She'd never eaten Brussels sprouts in her life. "I really had my doubts about coming here," she added, sounding a bit too adult for her age.

"Oh, Tori, you know we had to move after what Grandpa Harvey said."

Joe blanched. "That's enough, son," he cautioned, his voice more harsh than he'd intended. He saw Angelica's eyes widen with concern and tried lightening his voice for a change of subject. "This moussaka is really delicious, isn't it, kids?"

They both agreed, though with lackluster enthusiasm which, Joe felt sure, came from the way he had quashed Nick's comment. From the corner of his eye he saw how Angelica studied him, and he knew he ought to prepare to explain this small skeleton in the family closet.

It wasn't long before dinner and cleanup ended—again Joe was amazed by the smooth way Angelica organized everyone, eliciting the children's help without a single whine from them—and the kids settled down to play computer games in Angelica's office while she offered him a cool lemonade on the back porch swing. Joe remembered only too well how things had gone between them when they'd last sat on that swing, and he was determined not to let such things happen again. Still he knew Angelica was offering him an opportunity to talk, and he welcomed the lemonade and the cool evening air.

"You don't have to tell me about it if you don't want to, Joe," she began as she sat beside him.

"About what?" he asked. "You mean, about my father-in-law and the difficult situation that forced us to move away?"

"That was my allusion," she observed, somewhat dryly. "Obviously it's still an issue between you and the children."

"And between me and my in-laws," he added. Then he sighed. It would be good to share this burden with a sympathetic ear.

"It was just after my wife's funeral," he said, turning his thoughts so inward upon his own distraught emotions that he didn't see Angelica flinch at the word "wife." "We had the service in a huge church hall where my father-in-law is a regular contributor, then we followed in the funeral cortege to the cemetery and had a small graveside service there." He winced and Angelica laid her hand on top of his.

He patted her hand and continued. "Then there was a luncheon at my in-laws' home, with cold cuts and salads and everyone having a chance to mingle and chat and share memories of Roberta—" He paused, gulping back emotion. "—and tears."

Angelica stroked his hand. "You don't have to go on, Joe. You can stop here if you want to."

"No, I'm started now," he said, then took a deep breath and continued on a sigh. "The crowd was thinning and most of the well-wishers had gone away when I decided it was time for me to take my children home. I dreaded facing that cold, dark house all alone. I went up to my in-laws to thank them for all they'd done to get me and my kids through those first awful days. Nick and

Tori were both with me when my father-in-law said . . ."

Again he paused, the words stuck behind the knot in his throat. "Really, Joe," Angelica said. "You can quit now if you want to," and Joe realized she wasn't offering it; she was begging, hurting because he hurt and wanting him to stop.

"I'm sorry," he said, stopping, but then he saw her face change.

"I only want you to do whatever will make you feel better," she said. "If you want to tell me . . ."

"I didn't think I wanted to," he answered. "I thought I'd never want to share this with anyone, but now that you're listening . . ." He studied her face, looking for permission to continue.

She nodded. "Go ahead."

He swallowed a bitter chuckle. "I guess I have such a hard time repeating it because it struck me so hard at the time," he told her, "and because some part of me still can't help believing it. My father-in-law blames me for Roberta's death."

"No! Oh, no!" Angelica's face contorted in mixed horror and sympathy. "Oh, Joe, you mustn't blame yourself. How could he blame you?"

"He blamed me for everything—for not earning enough money to support my family so Roberta felt she needed to work part-time; for not providing a better road car, so she'd be protected in the event of a freeway accident; for letting her drive alone in heavy freeway traffic. He even blamed me for not loving her enough during the years we spent together."

"Oh, Joe." Angelica reached up to stroke his face, and he was tempted to fall into her arms, letting her hold him while he sobbed out his pain.

But it wasn't right to burden her with that, and he refused to do so. "It's okay," he croaked, his voice raw.

"No," she said, "it's not okay. It's probably understandable, though, in a way. I mean, the poor man had lost his daughter just as you lost your . . . your late wife. I expect he was distraught with grief, and angry about his loss. He probably didn't mean any of the awful things he said, but it's unfortunate that you were the one he chose to burden with his anger."

Joe turned his eyes up to meet hers, the pain written plainly on his face. "Always the sympathetic ear—hey, Angelica? Sympathy for my 'poor father-in-law,' for my children, just not—"

Angelica laid gentle fingers on his lips. "And for you, too," she said, before he could finish his sentence. "For you, especially." Then she leaned forward and replaced her fingers with her lips.

The kiss was simple, brief and warm, a mere brushing of her lips to his, but it sent such a rush of blood to Joe's head that he felt suddenly dizzy, and such a rush of heat to the rest of him that he wanted to sweep Angelica into his arms and kiss her until he had sated himself in her kisses, like a satyr drunk on old wine.

Not daring either, he simply waited for the few seconds until she pulled away, then watched the rosy flush steal across her features. "I'm sorry," she said uneasily. "That was far too bold of me. Honestly, I don't know what comes over me when I'm around you, Joe Vanetti. I seem to be willing to risk all kinds of things—"

"Hush," Joe said, succumbing to the temptation. He drew her into his arms and lowered her into his lap, kissing her as thoroughly as he'd wanted to for ages, as thoroughly as she seemed to need to be kissed, so thoroughly that he finally had to withdraw in order to breathe, or risk passing out on top of her. He caught his breath on a long sigh, and drew slowly away from her, helping her to sit straight again. "Now I'm the one who should apologize," he said.

She smiled, a gentle smile full of sympathy and patient understanding, a tantalizing smile filled with mischief. "Please, don't," she said, and snuggled into the curve of his arm. He smiled in answer, and let her.

For some time they sat that way, wrapped in each other's arms, enjoying the comfort of closeness, sipping at their lemonade as they let the swing pull them back and forth, forth and back, not worrying about their tomorrows but simply enjoying the pleasure of being together today.

And so their weeks settled into a pattern: dinner at Angelica's on Monday evening, with a foray into the garden afterward; Tori's violin lesson on Wednesday afternoons, after which Angelica sometimes came with them to watch the afternoon soccer game, sometimes followed by takeout supper in the park; dinner out on Friday evenings, with a separate dessert afterward, sometimes in the park and sometimes at the Vanetti home.

Joe had been reluctant at first to let Angelica see the bachelor-pad-with-kids that was his home. He had been surprised and gratified when she had complimented him on his choice of decor and on the orderly way he had arranged things. He had been careful not to mention that his wife had chosen the furniture and picked their color schemes.

Nor did he think too much about what might be happening with Angelica. She was a family friend, that was all. And if they occasionally held or kissed each other, whether on her porch swing, or on the bench in the public park, or even in his kitchen as he spooned Tori's half-baked first attempt at cake baking into bowls to be served with spoons . . . what of that? It didn't mean anything. Not everything had to be meaningful, did it?

It was on a Saturday evening, roughly a month after his arrival in Rainbow Rock, as he visited his sister's home following another of the kids' soccer games—this one far more organized—when Cretia cornered him in her kitchen. "Tell me about you and Angelica," she said.

Joe balked. "What makes you think there's anything to tell?"

"Don't play games with me, Joe. Your kids can hardly stop talking about her. It's 'Angelica this' and 'Angelica that' all the time with both Nick and Tori, and the things they say make it clear you spend a lot of time with her, several nights a week from what I gather."

"Yeah, well—" Joe began.

"Then again," Cretia went on, "there is the fact that I saw you kissing her last night as I drove by the park on my way home from work."

Joe felt his face grow warm. "Oh, that."

"Yeah, that." She waited.

He glanced away. "What's there to tell?"

"Offhand, I'd say there's quite a bit. From the sound of things, you're eating dinner at her house a couple of nights a week—"

"Just Mondays."

"Every Monday?"

"Well, yeah."

"And seeing her on Wednesdays for Tori's violin lessons—"

"Yeah, but that's just the lesson."

"And soccer afterward, and sometimes dinner, too."

"Okay, okay." Joe was growing petulant. "Soccer and sometimes dinner, too."

"Then there are the Friday evening dinners out—"

"How do you know—?"

"And occasional Saturdays at the second soccer game . . ."

"You're right. Okay, you're right. We are seeing a lot of each other."

"And how many of those evenings end in kisses like the one I saw last night?" Cretia was studying her brother.

Joe didn't like her look at all. "May I ask what business this is of yours? I mean, what does it matter to you whether I'm seeing Angelica, or kissing Angelica, or—"

"It doesn't matter at all," she answered lightly. "Except that you're my brother and I love you."

"Oh. That."

"Yes, oh that. And I care about Angelica, too. I don't want to see you getting in over your head before you're ready, and I don't want to see her hurt."

Joe felt his brows draw together. "What makes you think I'd hurt her?"

"I know you wouldn't mean to, Joe, but you know that good intentions make up the pavement on the road to—"

"Yeah, yeah. I've heard."

Cretia laid a hand on his arm. "You're a little like a man on the rebound. Roberta didn't mean to leave you, but left you she did, and you're alone and hurting. Some attention from a pretty woman is sure to make it all feel better, and Angelica is definitely a pretty woman."

"Are you kidding? She's beautiful."

Cretia's look grew more speculative. "Okay, beautiful," she said. "Which only goes to prove my point. Maybe you need to think a little about what you're doing, and what she is coming to mean to you. You've known her for most of your life, but you've really only spent time with her for about a month. You're getting in fairly deeply, fairly quickly, and that may not be good, for either of you."

"What are you afraid of, sis? Angelica is a grown woman. She can make her own choices."

"Yes, she can. But she's not like most of the grown women you know. She may be close to your own age, but she has the social experience of someone much, much younger." She gave Joe a pleading look, and he had the impression that she was hoping he'd fill in the blanks, so she wouldn't have to spell out what she was saying.

Joe knew which blanks she wanted him to fill in, but he resisted. He didn't like the image of himself he saw when he connected all the dots. "Yeah? So?" he asked, his voice belligerent.

"So I don't want to see you hurt each other, just because you're both alone and lonely." Cretia's voice was pointed. "Just be sure you know what you're doing," she said with a sigh, and returned to her other guests.

Late that night, long after he should have been asleep, Joe lay awake, examining his conscience. Was he using Angelica, as his sister had implied? Was he taking advantage of her inexperience, her gentle nature? He didn't think so. At least, he hadn't thought so before Cretia had cornered him in the kitchen this evening. Now he wasn't so certain. He knew he didn't want to stop seeing Angelica. He didn't want to stop kissing her, either. Then again, maybe that was part of the problem. He was still weighing the pros and cons when he finally fell into a fitful rest.

Across town, Angelica DeForest lay in her own bed, thinking about the hazards of boldness. Joe Vanetti and his children were fast becoming an intricate part of her life, so deeply interwoven into the fabric of her days and evenings that she feared that fabric would simply fall apart, threadbare, if Joe ever attempted to extricate himself and his family from her world. And Angelica was surprised at herself, at the way she was pursuing Joe, at the rules she was breaking now, rules that she'd been taught with such care all her life.

Oh, there were some rules that went beyond breaking, some that drove to the fiber of her moral core, rules she would not break, not for anyone. They were too much a part of who and what she was. But the social rules her mother and grandmother had taught with such infinite care and precision . . . Well, as far as she could tell, there were a number of those rules that deserved to be broken.

She lay there in her bed, counting them off with some pleasure. *Never wear trousers.* Ha! That one had died an early death. Since that first Saturday picnic at Cretia's house, she seldom saw Joe when she wore a skirt, except sometimes at church. *Never kiss a man.* She'd broken that one, eagerly, on the night Joe had told her about the strain with his in-laws, and why he'd felt he had to move back to Rainbow Rock. He hadn't seemed to mind, and *she* certainly hadn't. *Never call a man.* She'd broken that one just last week, when she'd invited herself to the Saturday soccer game a week ago. *Keep a man guessing. Never tell him how much he means to you.* She'd slaughtered that one several times since Joe had come back to town, and she intended to keep breaking it, whenever and however Joe needed her support. She was coming to care for Joe Vanetti—not just for the remarkable boy athlete she had once worshiped, but for the complex, tender man she was coming to know—and love.

Chapter Six

"Thank you, Angelica. The lemon sorbet was delicious. In fact, the whole meal was wonderful—as usual." It was Monday evening, and Joe was in Angelica's kitchen, helping her clean up after their meal together, the kids already busy with her office computer.

"You're welcome," she answered, accepting the fond kiss he placed on her cheek. "I hope it won't hurt your feelings if I observe that you seem tired tonight."

He slipped his arms around her, cradling her back against his chest. "Tough day, I guess," he said, burying his face in her hair.

She leaned into his touch, then spoke over her shoulder. "Want to tell me about it?"

Joe sighed. "Not much to tell, really. It's just tough sometimes, being the staff gadfly."

"Gadfly?" She drew away enough that she could look

into his eyes. "I've heard that expression, but I can't say I know what it means."

"A true gadfly is a big critter," Joe explained, measuring its length between his thumb and forefinger, "the kind that annoys large animals like horses or cattle. Though its bite isn't dangerous, it's definitely annoying. That's why any really obnoxious or irritating person is called a gadfly."

"Joe! You're not obnoxious!"

"Not to you, maybe." He shrugged. "At work, it's my job to annoy people."

She drew her brows together. "I don't understand."

"It's pretty simple when you think about it. I mean, I'm hired by the company, but it's my job to keep an eye on the company. If Sam Watson needs to improve the tolerances for the boiler intake valves, I'm the one who has to spot the problem and bug him about it. If Rudy Velasquez needs to build another loop into the cooling chamber to ensure that the water going into the lake isn't too hot, again I'm the guy who catches it and needles Rudy until he gets the job done. It's the same way for the groundskeepers and the fellows who decide where the coal is dumped and stored, and every other part of the plant. If there's a problem, it's my job to catch it. Then I annoy every other part of the plant operation, and every other person who works there, until the problem gets fixed. Nobody is ever happy to see me coming."

"Ummm. I can see how that could be difficult," Angelica observed. "Was there a special problem today?"

Joe nodded. "A big one. I can't talk about it for proprietary reasons—plant security and all that. Suffice to say that if we hadn't gotten this one straightened out, the next step was emergency shutdown."

"Ooh." Angelica appreciated the severity of that announcement. "I don't think the plant has gone on emergency shutdown more than twice in all the years I've lived here."

"If it had, you shouldn't have known it," Joe said. "Things are set up so that if a shutdown becomes necessary, the power flow will be uninterrupted and repairs effected quickly. But you're right," he added, taking another small slice of the lemon-cheese bars Angelica had served with the sorbet, "shutdown is a rare thing. It doesn't happen often."

"So things were rough today," Angelica concluded.

"Yeah," he said wearily, "pretty rough."

"Well," she said, and there was something pointed about her voice. "At least you'll have tomorrow to recover."

He looked confused. "Huh?"

"The Fourth of July. You have the holiday off, right?"

He raised an eyebrow. "I'd almost forgotten. Today was such a rough one, I think I forgot all about the calendar."

"But you do have the holiday off?"

He nodded. "Yeah, I do." It took him a minute to catch on to the fact she was hinting. Once he caught on, he was embarrassed he hadn't thought of it before. "Would you like to share the day with us?"

Angelica grinned, practically purring with satisfaction. "Sounds good. What are you planning?"

"The kids and I are going to sleep in late, I think." He yawned, as if to emphasize the need. "Then I plan to take a picnic out to Chevlon Canyon."

"Chevlon? I haven't been there since high school."

"Then maybe it's time you went again. I'm not going to do anything fancy for the food. I'll probably just pick up fried chicken and fixin's at the supermarket deli."

"Would you like me to bring something?"

"Just yourself." He drew her back into his embrace, drinking solace from her presence.

"Are you sure, Joe? I could easily bake a cake, or—"

"Really, Angelica. Let us handle the food this time. It will be good for you to just relax and enjoy the day."

"Are you planning to swim?" she asked. "I mean, should I plan to bring a swimming suit, or a change of clothes?"

Joe paused, momentarily distracted by the idea of Angelica in a bathing suit. "If you'd like," he said. "I expect the kids are just going to wear cutoffs and T-shirts. We'll bring some towels so everyone can be wet and dry in the same clothes."

"That sounds fine. Then in the evening? For the fireworks?"

"We're going into Holbrook with Max and Cretia and the kids. I think a bunch of the McAllisters are going at the same time, so we'll probably all park close together, but Max is taking his big van, so there should be plenty of room. You're welcome to join us if you'd like."

"Great. I'd like that." She snuggled warmly against him, vaguely wondering if this was how love felt.

The holiday dawned clear and cool, and Angelica was up early, tending to her gardens. She had harvested less last night than was usual for a Monday evening, and her garden was producing more with each passing day. She prepared a couple of boxes of fresh produce to deliver to neighbors with large families who lived on her block, then took a few things to her other neighbors. She also cut two bouquets of fresh flowers for her dining table and the small table near the grand piano in her parlor. These two bouquets, filled with roses and fresh lavender, should keep her house aromatic and fresh for several days to come.

Though the clinic in Holbrook had treated patients the day before, there were none today because of the holiday. She would do yesterday's transcription tomorrow morning, the way she usually did Friday's work on a Monday, taking the holiday off. By 10:00, she was dressed and ready to go, plaid shorts and a T-shirt on under her jeans and long-sleeved cotton shirt. She knew not to expect the Vanettis before eleven, but she couldn't help being eager. She'd always loved Chevlon Canyon— a place as timeless and unchanging as any she had ever seen—and she very much looked forward to sharing it with Joe and his family.

True to his word, Joe appeared just at eleven, driving a high-bottomed, four-wheel-drive sport utility vehicle, which he'd borrowed from one of the McAllisters. Angelica tossed her bag in the back, greeted Tori and Nick, and soon they were on their way south toward Holbrook, then down I-40 toward Joseph City, then along a named road toward an unnamed one that wound onto private property, wending their way until they finally came to an off-road trail where they followed the tracks of countless earlier explorers over bare, dun-colored stone, bouncing and jostling toward the canyon one of the first explorers had named for himself.

"We're here," Joe called as he brought the truck to a halt, apparently in the middle of nowhere.

It's a good thing I've been to Chevlon before, Angelica thought as she helped the children separate out the few parcels they'd brought with picnic goods and cameras in them. *Otherwise, I'd be as confused as Tori looks right now.* As if to prove her point, Tori chose that minute to ask, "Dad, where are we? I thought you said there was a canyon here."

Joe grinned. "There is," he said simply. "Follow me." He walked slightly ahead as Angelica, Tori, and Nick followed behind. And then he took a step downward where there appeared to be no downward step. A moment later, his head disappeared below the sandstone. The children watched, wide-eyed, until they stepped closer and saw the canyon trail dropping away precipitously below them. This was an illusion Angelica had always enjoyed, and marveled at. From only a few feet away, the yellow-dun sandstone on this side of the canyon seemed to meld seamlessly with the yellow-dun sandstone on the opposite side. It was only when one was actually upon the canyon—in fact, almost falling into it—that one finally saw it: the mesquites and piñon pines, the deep blue waters of the creek as it carved its way through the sandstone walls and over the rough sands, the perfect symmetry of the deep, cool holes and faster shallows.

"Come on," Angelica said, eager to join Joe. "Let's follow." She encouraged Tori to go first, then Nick, herself bringing up the rear so she'd be certain each of the children made it safely. At the bottom, Joe waited to give them each a hand down, over the last tricky steps where their feet might have slipped on the loose pebbles near the bottom.

"Easy," he cautioned his daughter. "Take it easy," he said to his son. "Here, let me help you," he told Angelica, putting his hands on either side of her slender waist and lifting her to the canyon floor. Then he kept one hand at her waist as they walked into the shade of a nearby overhang and spread a blanket on the silty beach.

Angelica sank down onto the cool, silty beaches of the canyon, drinking deeply of the water-freshened air. Here, only thirty-some feet below the baking heat of the yellow sandstone, the temperature was at least twenty degrees cooler. In fact, in this shady part of the canyon, she was glad she'd worn a long-sleeved shirt, though memory told her she'd be grateful for the cool swimming holes before the afternoon had passed.

Joe worked busily, spreading the feast he'd purchased at the deli that morning: fried chicken, potato and macaroni salads, a watermelon, cookies. . . . Knowing Angelica would join them, he'd also brought a bowl full of mixed salad greens, some cherries and grapes and baby carrots. Angelica smiled knowingly as he set them before her. "Trying to please a vegetarian appetite?"

"Or maybe just a more discriminating one." He spread paper plates and poured lemonade into cups, then called the kids to join them. Tori and Nick, who had just spotted a lizard sunning himself on a rock and had harried the poor creature until it hid itself in the crack of a large stone, quickly hurried to eat. "I'll offer a blessing," Joe said.

Angelica hadn't mentioned anything, but she'd noticed the way Joe had hesitated before the first time he offered a prayer in her home. She felt happy for him that he seemed to find it so much easier now. She basked in the sound of his voice as he thanked the Almighty for good food, good company, and pleasant surroundings. Then he concluded his prayer and began serving food to his hungry family. *And me*, Angelica reminded herself sternly. *His family and me. I mustn't forget I'm here by invitation only.* She suppressed a sigh. When she was with them like this, as she was so often lately, it would have been easy to believe she was one of the family, not just a family friend. *Is that what you want, Angelica?* This time she sighed. Wasn't it what she had always wanted? Throughout the long, lonely years, the one thing she had wanted most was a husband and children of her own.

"Are you all right?" Joe asked, watching her with concern.

"I'm fine." She didn't mention that the right words from him would make her feel ever so much better.

While she nibbled on carrots and cherries, salad greens, and even a small piece of chicken, she watched the family interact around her and thought of what it would mean to be a permanent part of their lives. Introspective as always, she challenged herself frequently. Was she really in love, or was she just moved by the convenience of having an attractive man close, and apparently interested in her? Did she really want the children, too? Or was she only pleased by the children because they were came with the man? Was it really Joe Vanetti she wanted, or was it the powerful young man who'd been the idol of her youth?

The questions may have been tough, but answering them was easy. Angelica DeForest, who'd never been in love in her life, was in love now. Definitely. Wildly.

Deeply and truly. She wanted Joe Vanetti, and she wanted Nick and Tori, too. *I love you, Joe. I love you, Tori. I love you, Nick. I love you, Joe. I love you, Joe.* She sat thinking the words at them, willing them to hear and feel, to share and return her love.

Mid-afternoon on the Fourth of July and Joe lazed against the sun-warmed sandstone beside one of Chevlon's best swimming holes, watching with undisguised pleasure as Angelica swam and dunked and splashed his children, reveling in their play. *She's beautiful*, he thought again as he had so often lately. *So very beautiful.* Today she was an angel in bright plaid shorts and a lemon yellow T-shirt, wet cotton clinging to the oh-so-feminine curves of her perfect form, outlining every delicious, touchable curve. As he watched, the angel squealed and splashed Nick, then dove headfirst into the deepest swirls of the swimming hole before he could retaliate, emerging a moment later looking drenched and gorgeous, a veritable Venus rising from the sea.

You've been alone too long, he told himself, trying to counter the effect watching her was having on his rising temperature, on his already-battered self-restraint. She'd been so available, and so easy to get to know. Convenient. Comfortable. Joe felt like kicking himself. He wasn't in love. Of course he wasn't. Love was what he had felt for Roberta, and no one else. Never before and never since. But it was easy and pleasant and sometimes, like now, even fun to be around Angelica.

Is that so wrong? he asked himself, but the guilt he was already feeling told him the truth. He was taking advantage of someone who'd been good and kind and loving toward him and his needy children. He was enjoying the comfort and convenience of having an attractive, caring woman near. *It's wrong*, he chided himself. *It's wrong and you know it, especially since she may well be falling in love with you.*

The selfish part of him knew that was convenient, too. If Angelica was in love, that would make it all the easier to take advantage of her feelings. He could enjoy her comfort and kindness, her nearness, her good cooking, the nurturing she provided his children, even a few tender kisses offered and relished. He could revel in her warmth and beauty, her nurture and love, and never have to relinquish his heart. *But you're a cad if you do.* Joe sighed.

What if I married her? The thought occurred to him like a bolt out of the clear blue sky above him, the slice of it that showed at the top of the canyon mirrored in the waters of the creek. *She'd have my name, my children, my home. I'd provide for her, so she wouldn't have to transcribe records or teach music lessons unless she wanted to.* In that moment, it seemed like the perfect idea.

But is it really fair? he asked, more critical now. He would have the comfort and convenience of a warm, willing companion, someone to cook and clean, to help him mother his children, to hear his desperation when he felt sorely in need of comfort, to hold him when he was so desperately alone in the dark of the night. And what would she get? A man who needed her, but didn't love her, whose love was dead and buried. A man who wanted her, but offered so little of himself in return.

A woman like Angelica needs to be loved, deserves to be loved. He wriggled uncomfortably against the now-too-warm stone. Married to him, used because she was convenient, loving and knowing she was not loved in return, she'd slowly wither and die. *The way my children were withering before they met her.* Joe's mood darkened, then blackened, as he watched the angel who played splash with his children, the Venus who played havoc with his heart.

"Is that what I think it is?" Angelica leaned forward, not quite touching the engraving scratched into the rock walls of the canyon.

"Native petroglyphs," Joe answered. "There are thousands of them in the canyon."

"I guess I'd forgotten that." She settled back into the crook of his arm.

Joe nestled her against him, aware he would have to forego this pleasure in the future, but wanting it far too much to be willing to forego it now. "There are better ones farther along this way. Want to see them?"

Angelica looked back over her shoulder, in the direction they'd come from. "Should we check on the children?"

"We've only been away a few minutes," Joe answered. "We're not far from them, and I'm sure they can find us if they need to."

"Okay, then." She smiled, a trusting look that made him feel like a heel. "Let's see those petroglyphs."

"This way." *Okay, so I'm a heel,* Joe added to himself, *but I want this time with her, this quiet moment. If I'm going to be fair to her, I'll have to be more distant in the future, but today . . . today we're here and we're together. At least I can have this.* He led the way around a sharp turn in the canyon's maze. At least two distinct turns now separated them from his children. They were alone, as alone as if they were the only two in the world. For a moment, he was going to let his imagination enjoy that idea.

"Look," he said, pointing upward. Some ancient artist had left his mark upon the canyon's stone walls. Swirls and human figures mixed with lightning strikes and the shapes of animals.

"Wow!" Angelica stared in awe. "I had no idea there was so much of this here."

"The petroglyphs in this canyon are the best examples in this part of the state," Joe answered. "Even better than those on Picture Rock, in the Petrified Forest."

"I've certainly never seen better ones." Angelica inclined her head to study the pictures far above her. "How do you suppose the artist got up there?"

"I've wondered that myself. And I really couldn't guess. I'd say it's likely he used toeholds and leaned against the rock just below it, right there." He pointed. "Or maybe he hung down on a rope suspended from the rocks at the canyon's mouth."

Angelica looked upward to the place Joe indicated. "How do you know it was a he?" she asked, mischief dancing in her eyes.

"I don't, of course. I just assumed that anyone with that much time on his hands was probably a man. The women always seemed to be busy cooking and tanning, tending children and crops."

She grinned. "You certainly weaseled your way out of that one."

He grinned back. "I've always been good at thinking on my feet." Then he took her elbows, and his expression changed. "Come here," he said, his voice suddenly grown husky.

She looked over her shoulder, in the direction where his children waited. "Are you sure this is a good idea?"

"I don't want to think about that just now," he answered honestly. "I just want to kiss you. And I hope you'll kiss me back."

She sighed, melting into him. "I expect I probably will," she said, and tipped her head back in a most alluring gesture.

Joe groaned, a tortured sound made low in his throat, and took what she offered, crushing her against him while he ravished her mouth, firmly stilling his conscience, telling himself he was *not* taking advantage as long as she enjoyed it, too. When he finally had to come up for air, he continued holding her tightly against him while the trembling in his limbs subsided, holding her until he felt he could speak again. "You're delicious," he murmured into her fragrant, still-damp hair. "Absolutely delicious."

"I love . . ." she began, then he saw her face flush a deep scarlet color. "I love it when you kiss me like that," she said.

"I do, too," Joe answered, but he couldn't lie to himself any longer. That wasn't what Angelica had started to say. He *was* taking advantage, and he *wasn't* being fair. He needed to end this before it could go any farther. "Much as I hate to admit it," he said, releasing his hold, "I think we need to get back to the children."

"All right," she said, though he thought he heard a touch of disappointment in her voice. "Race you?" She primed for a quick start.

"Nah, I'd lose," he said, giving one more admiring look to her long, long legs.

"Ah, come on," she teased. "Ready, set—"

"You run; I'll watch." He grinned wickedly.

She flushed. "Okay. If you're going to be that way about it . . ." She took his hand, walking at his side.

He tried to tell himself she was a good family friend, just a friend walking along beside him, a friend holding his hand. It didn't seem to matter that he knew it was a lie.

"Tori, you carried the big bag, right? And Nick, you get this one. Okay, there. I think we've got everything." Angelica helped load the remains of the picnic. She took one bag of leftover food and another full of damp, well-used towels for herself. "Last one to the top is a rotten egg!" she called, sprinting for the path that would allow them to climb out of the canyon and back to their car. *Let Joe bring up the rear this time.*

"Right behind you!" Tori called.

"I'm next!" Nick added.

"Looks like I'm the goat this time," Joe said, apparently content with that role as he picked up the ice chest and another bag and willingly followed the group.

"No, Daddy," Tori clarified. "Not the goat, the rotten egg!"

"Okay, so I'm the rotten egg."

The last word faded out for Angelica as she crested the canyon trail and emerged on the dun-yellow sandstone. It was like leaving Eden and entering another world entirely—a poorer world, and a much warmer one. Sweat broke out on her brow within seconds. She'd gone from paradise into . . . well, someplace much less pleasant. As she jogged for the truck, she smothered the sensation that the same thing had just happened in her relationship with Joe.

And I almost blew it, she thought, aghast at herself for the declaration she had very nearly made. *Thank goodness I recovered quickly.* That recovery had allowed her to hang on to a little piece of her self-esteem, some small part of herself that Joe Vanetti hadn't yet branded his.

She ran the last few steps to the sports vehicle and threw her bags in the back, then slipped into the front passenger seat, waiting for the others to catch up. Breaking rules was one thing. Declarations of deep emotion? That was something else again. She didn't need Grandma Poppy's Rules of Dating to tell her that. All she needed was the pleading of her own heart. Already suffering from insecurity, her heart begged her not to let down the last few defenses it had. For if she declared her feelings to Joe, and he didn't return them . . . She sighed, trying not to picture that sad image. Her poor heart had waited so long to love. Didn't it deserve to be loved in turn?

I'll wait, she declared to herself. *I'll wait until Joe says it first.*

And what if he doesn't? she asked. *What if he doesn't feel as I do?* Tears jumped into her eyes and she forced them down, unwilling to make a spectacle of herself by crying in front of Joe's children.

So what do I do about tonight? Joe had finished putting away the leftover food and organizing the rest of the things they'd taken into the canyon. It was more than an hour now since he'd dropped Angelica at her home and already he was in a panic. He'd almost blown it there in the canyon, had very nearly taken unfair advantage of a sweet and unsophisticated heart that deserved better than he had to give.

But I've already invited her for tonight. There's nothing to be done about that.

No, there was nothing to be done about that. And didn't that absolve him of the responsibility to try to do something? He grinned. *You're pretty good at rationalizing, aren't you, Vanetti?* But rationalization or not, he had already invited her and there really was nothing to be done about it now. So he'd pick her up around eight, as he'd promised, and keep her with his family group when they met up with Max and Cretia, then with the larger McAllister family. He'd keep his children nearby as chaperones this time, along with the Carmodys and the assorted McAllisters, and that would help him avoid the temptation to get her alone again despite what he wanted, despite what he always wanted when he was near her now. They'd enjoy the fireworks tonight and he'd see her home while the children were still with them, then he'd come up with an excuse for why they couldn't have dinner with her on Friday, or come back to her house again on Monday evening.

Slowly, slowly, he'd begin to wean himself and his children away from her tenderness, her sweetness, her willing touch. She'd probably be hurt, but it would be easier on her than if things went the other way. Wouldn't it?

Tired of trying to fathom the world within Angelica's heart, he set about the task of making sure his children had had enough to eat.

He opened the refrigerator and found it full of produce from Angelica's garden. He opened the bread box and found a loaf of her home-baked raisin-cinnamon bread.

He opened the pantry and found three jars of homemade jam she'd sent back with his family last week.

Joe sighed and left the kitchen, slamming the pantry door behind him. Extricating Angelica from his life might just be more difficult than he thought.

Chapter Seven

"**O**h, look! I think we're getting started." Angelica crooned her approval as the first rocket burst in the darkening sky above them. She sat on a rough woolen army blanket, spread over bales of straw on the back of a huge flatbed truck. Chris McAllister, the youngest of the McAllister brothers and the one who still ran the family pig farm, had outfitted the flatbed just for this occasion with straw bales and warm blankets and a couple of ice chests filled with good things to drink. Now the whole McAllister family, as well as some who weren't McAllisters, were spread across the flatbed, preparing to enjoy the show.

Kate McAllister Richards was there, with her new husband, Wiley. Joan, the oldest child, had brought her husband, Bob Ross, and their four children. Jim McAllister and his wife, Meg, had their toddling daughter, Alexis, and Kurt McAllister was there with wife Alexa. Chris had brought his wife, Sarah, and their newlywed friends, Logan Redhorse and his wife, Eden.

Max Carmody, half-brother to Meg McAllister, was considered part of the clan, and since Cretia was a producer for Rainbow Productions—owned by Meg and her brother-in-law, Kurt—she was also invited to family gatherings in her own right, along with Lydia and Danny. That was how Joe came to hook up with the McAllisters, by virtue of being related to Max and Cretia. Alexa had explained all this to Angelica during the first few minutes after she'd joined them, while people were still jockeying for space.

"It makes quite a group," Alexa had concluded, just before the fireworks began.

"I can see that," Angelica had answered. She'd counted close to thirty people in the McAllister contingent.

Funny, she thought to herself now as she watched first one showy burst of fire, then another. *When we were all in school together, the McAllister kids, from the pig farm, were the only folks lower on the social ladder than poor, dumb Angelica. Just look at them now!* The McAllisters had grown into handsome, confident, charming adults with beautiful families, and there was no question, based on the welcoming comments from other people around them at the fireworks display, that they had taken an entirely different position in the social structure of this small town. People clearly looked up to and admired the McAllisters.

Angelica watched with fascination as one group, then another, came to greet the self-contained community on the back of their flatbed truck. The people of Rainbow Rock had not just accepted the pig farmer's children;

they'd moved them into leadership positions. *If it can happen to the McAllisters, maybe even poor, dumb Angelica has a chance. . . .*

"Come here and cuddle, wife," Jim said, drawing Meg close to his side. Around them on the flatbed, Jim and Meg snuggled, as did Bob and Joan, Kurt and Alexa, Chris and Sarah, Logan and Eden, Max and Cretia . . . even Kate and Wiley. Angelica slanted a suggestive look at Joe, who seemed not to notice. She wondered if it was just the people who surrounded them, if he was more circumspect in a crowd. Or maybe he regretted his earlier impulse? She didn't want to think so, but he'd been somewhat more distant ever since that moment in the canyon when she'd almost revealed herself—distant and somehow more tense. Even now the tension she felt radiating from him was almost enough to curdle her stomach.

"Ah!" she cried as a series of rockets burst above them, red and gold fire lighting the night. The outburst allowed a release of the terrible tension inside her, a tension so great, she longed to scream.

Look at her. Just look at her. She's exquisite. Joe watched Angelica from the corner of his eye, stealing glimpses of her and hoping no one caught him looking. It was nearing evening when he'd dropped her at her home, damp and tousled, her skin flush with sunlight, her lips still slightly swollen. Now only a couple of hours later, she sat beside him—perfectly made up, perfectly coiffed, perfect. In fact, she looked so put together, so utterly composed, that he'd have sworn he'd just witnessed The Return of the Ice Queen. That is, he'd have sworn it until that look she'd just flashed him, the one that suggested since everyone else was cuddling, they should, too.

Oh, what a temptation you are, sweet Angelica! He yearned toward her as she leaned against his arm. Joe could feel her warmth even through the layers of shirt and jacket they both wore, and he longed to hold her close. But it wasn't just the several dozen curious eyes around them that caused him to keep his place. He didn't love her, and Angelica deserved to be loved.

I'm doing the right thing, he assured himself. *I'm doing the thing that will be best for her, best for all of us in the long run. I've let this go too far already.* But as he watched her eyes light up with the fire from the sky, her hair shine in the light of the rockets and the stars, he couldn't help wondering if maybe there wasn't some acceptable compromise, some answer that would be fair to her and still allow him to stay close enough to admire her, near enough to touch her once in a while.

"You know, our family has a long history with these fireworks," Jim was saying. There had been a brief pause in the program as one of the huge ground displays on the bluff above them burned out.

"Tell us, Uncle Jim." It was Alice, Joan and Bob's eldest.

"This fireworks display was the first place I brought Meg when she came back to town a few years ago."

"That's right," Meg agreed. "Jim was the town's most eligible bachelor. We sat in the back of his truck and the women kept coming out of nowhere, flouncing around in front of him and checking out the competition. It was downright embarrassing."

Jim chuckled fondly and kissed his wife's hair. "As I

recall, even Cretia stopped in to say 'hi,' " he teased, apparently trying to get a rise out of Cretia.

It worked. "I was just being sociable," Cretia demurred. "Besides, Meg's brother hadn't come to visit yet, so I had yet to discover what a real man was like."

"Oooh," the group chorused.

Jim chuckled again. "Touché," he said, acknowledging the hit.

"Speak for yourself," Meg said. "I'm just glad you don't know what you're missing." She kissed her husband soundly and again the group aahed their approval.

"Logan and I don't have those memories," Eden said as she prodded her husband. "He was supposed to come to the fireworks with a group of us the night Chris and Sarah were married, but he stood us all up."

"Those were the days when I was still trying to avoid you," Logan explained sweetly, "before I knew what a blessing you'd be in my life."

"Ah, how sweet," Eden said. "You got away with that one, honey," and she kissed him.

All the kissing was making Angelica edgy. "So this is your first anniversary?" she asked Chris and Sarah.

"That's right," Sarah answered. "We thought it would be fun to be married on the Fourth of July, both of us taking dependents on Independence Day."

"At least I'm not likely to forget our anniversary," Chris answered, and Sarah responded, "You'd better not," while the people around them kidded and teased.

"We came here that night," Cretia said. "That is, last year, the night you two were married, Max and I brought Lydia and Marcie and Danny to the fireworks."

"That's right," Max answered. "That's when we saw our night rainbow."

"Night rainbow?" Angelica asked.

"Uh-huh," Cretia answered. The group was momentarily distracted by another barrage of bright green and silver in the sky, then Cretia continued. "We'd both been married before, and for several weeks we'd been telling our kids that the possibility of either of us marrying again was about as likely as their chances of finding a rainbow in the night sky. Then at the fireworks that night, they found one."

"A rainbow?" Angelica asked, confused.

"Well, a ground display of a rainbow," Max said. "Look, there it is now." Even as they spoke, the fire crew was lighting another ground display, this one in the shape of a seven-hued rainbow, bending across the upper edge of the bluff.

"After that," Cretia said, "well . . . the rest, as they say, is history."

"That's charming," Angelica answered, enjoying the lively camaraderie of this group.

"You two had better be careful," Kurt announced, clearly speaking to Joe and Angelica. "There's a history of romance here."

Angelica waited for Joe to respond, but he said nothing, almost as if he hadn't heard Kurt speak. "I'll be careful," Angelica said, speaking for herself only, and the group chuckled again as the rainbow above them burned out.

"So that's next Sunday after church. You'll join us, won't you?" Alexa had just invited Joe and his family, Angelica included, to join them at the weekly McAllister family dinner. "We meet at the family farm a little after one. That gives everyone time to go home and change clothes after church, and to pick up whatever dishes they're bringing to the potluck."

"What can I bring?" Angelica asked, speaking only for herself since Joe had not yet answered. His refusal to answer had seemed rather pointed.

"I'm not sure," Alexa said, then turning to her sister-in-law, "Meg, what do we still need for dinner Sunday?"

"How about a casserole and a salad?"

"Sounds good," Alexa answered. "Think you can manage that?"

"Sure," Angelica said.

"We'll see you Sunday, then."

"Sunday it is." Angelica waved as they broke away from the McAllister contingent, headed for Max's car.

That's when Max said, "Angelica, we'll have to pass by your house in order to take Joe's family back to their place. Do you mind if we just drop you on the way?"

Angelica paused only briefly before responding, "No, not at all." She hoped her disappointment didn't show in her voice.

It had been a lovely evening except for Joe's sudden coolness. She had enjoyed the fireworks display, and the company of the McAllister family. She had enjoyed almost everything except being so close to Joe, and having him ignore her. A few minutes later, as she got out of Max's car in front of her home, she waved good-bye to the mixed Carmodys and Vanettis, wondering what had happened.

Already Joe had told her he and the kids would be unable to invite her to dinner this coming Friday, or to join her at her home the next Monday evening. He had begged off, citing "other commitments," but she had the feeling his only other commitments were promises to himself, promises to get some distance from her. She couldn't help wondering what she might have done to offend him. Whatever it was, she wished to heaven she could take it back.

As she lay alone in her quiet bed, hoping for a restful sleep that would not come, she thought again of the way he had kissed her in the canyon. *Oh, to have that back again. To have him with me every day and every night.* Was marriage really too much to expect? Other people married and had families. True, Angelica had never been like other people, but she could aspire to this small slice of happiness, couldn't she? Sighing, she turned her face to the wall.

Joe worked his way along the catwalk around the boiler's superstructure, taking samples for the air quality tests he'd run later in the lab, working with only half a brain. *So far, so good*, he thought with the other half, the half that seemed permanently fixed on Angelica, and the problems in their budding relationship.

He'd begun the process of separating himself and his children from the lovely lady with the sky-blue eyes and the golden hair, the silvery voice of a saint and the beauty of a temptress. Already she'd sensed the tension and tentativeness in him. Already she was being hurt by it.

Better for her to hurt a little now, he rationalized, sure in his heart that if he let things continue the way they had been going, she'd end up married to him and hating him for it. *But I'm done with using her*, he told himself firmly. *My conscience won't allow me to go on like this any longer.*

When he heard the alarm bells going off like mad, he

thought for a moment that they, too, were in his head, that the alarms were telling him he was making a huge mistake. But the alarms weren't in his head; of course not. They were sounding all over the power plant, and he was the one who had to fix them. Snapping his brain into gear, he ran for the central office.

I should have realized, he thought minutes later, as he dashed from station to station, working madly to solve the problems his own calculations had caused before the entire plant had to be shut down. A power plant was a delicate system. Tinker with one part, you were likely to have unforeseeable consequences somewhere else. The quick fixes the crews had used on Monday to solve the problems he'd caught then were backfiring on him now in ways he never would have guessed, in ways that were going to keep him busy for hours to come.

And today is Tori's violin lesson. Drat! At least this would give him the opportunity to distance even more from the lovely lady he longed to hold.

Angelica had just returned from her run to the clinic in Holbrook, taking back the entries she'd transcribed that morning. She had changed into her gardening clothes and was getting ready to go into the backyard when the phone rang. "Hello?"

"Angelica, it's Joe."

Angelica took a deep, nerve-steadying breath before responding coolly, "Hi, Joe. How is your day going?"

"Awful," he answered. "Just awful. Remember I told you we had problems here on Monday?"

"I remember." She thought she remembered every word he'd ever said to her since they were both in junior high.

"Well, it's a whole lot worse today."

"Worse than emergency shutdown?" She had trouble imagining that.

"We didn't shut down on Monday, and we're trying to avoid it today, too," Joe answered. "But it's going to keep me here much of the night, or at very least, all evening."

"Sorry to hear that," she answered, trying to play it cool. Was this emergency real, or was it just another attempt to avoid her?

"I'm afraid that means I won't be bringing Tori for her lesson. I'm sorry about that, but I really can't get away."

She paused only briefly before deciding that, whatever the problems Joe had found in their relationship, they needn't have an impact on his daughter. "I can pick her up," she offered.

"I can't ask you to do that—"

"You didn't. I volunteered. Where is she?" Angelica picked up pen and paper, ready to note the address.

"She's at Cretia's house. Lydia is baby-sitting. But really, it wouldn't be fair for you—"

"Okay. I'll pick her up there."

"You don't need to do that."

"I know, but I don't mind. In fact, why don't I pick up both Tori and Nick? Nick can play computer games while Tori has her lesson, then I can feed them both dinner. We'll have something ready for you, too, when you come to get them later."

"Angelica, I can't allow that—" Joe began.

"I insist," she answered, then hung up before he could say more. When the phone rang again, almost immediately, she pretended she'd already left. She wasn't going to let Joe dictate how she related to his children when she was only doing what she'd done all along. He was *paying* her for the lessons, for goodness' sake. Wasn't this the least she could do?

Feeling somewhat smug about the way she'd handled things—boldness could pay off, after all—Angelica got into her car and drove toward the Carmody home.

It was nearing 9:00 when Joe finally left the power plant and drove toward Angelica's home. He had tried to head her off by calling Cretia's, but apparently one or another of the kids was on the Internet. The phone rang steadily busy each time he tried to get through. After three tries, the emergency at the plant had forced him back to the problems at hand, and he'd given up trying to stop her.

Here I've sworn not to take advantage of her, he ruminated as he drove down the road toward Holbrook, then north toward Rainbow Rock, *and she's picking my kids up at Cretia's house and feeding them dinner.* It soothed his conscience a little that she had volunteered for the task. *But she probably only volunteered because she thinks there's a future for us,* he told himself firmly. *You can't go on allowing this, Vanetti.*

Not that he'd allowed it this time. Joe couldn't stop the smile. He still felt stymied, and mildly admiring, of the way Angelica had manipulated him on the phone today. This wasn't the shy but intimidating girl he'd known during their school days. A new Angelica had emerged since he'd returned to Rainbow Rock—a strong, confident woman who knew what she wanted— and he found he rather liked her like this.

He pulled up in front of Angelica's home and loped

up her front walk. "Knock, knock," he announced as he opened the door.

"Who's there?" an angel voice answered, and Joe decided to play along.

"Joe," he said.

"Joe who?" Angelica had come into the living room and he could see her crossing toward the front door.

"Joe mama," he declared in a tough-guy voice, and Angelica chuckled.

"We really need to work on your repertoire of knock-knock jokes," she teased as she closed the door behind him, her hand just brushing his back.

He warmed instantly at the slight touch. "I thought that was pretty good," Joe defended. "You even laughed. Don't deny it. I saw you."

"I only laughed to be sociable," she said, then she directed him toward the kitchen. "Come on. We saved dinner for you."

"Really, Angelica. You've done too much already. Let me just pick up the kids and go."

Angelica answered with an airy tone. "You can do that if you want to, but the food is already waiting in the microwave. It's nourishing and reasonably tasty and it can be hot and ready in two minutes. If you don't eat it, I'll just have to put it into my compost pile." She waited.

Slowly, he allowed himself a grin. "You're pretty persuasive, you know that?"

Her grin was larger. "I know." She left him in the living room while she went into the kitchen to start the microwave. Somewhere along the way she must have said something to the children because seconds later they came bounding out of her office, eager to greet him.

"Hi, Dad!" Nick flung himself at his father for a big hug.

"You're kind of late tonight, Daddy," Tori said, giving him a smaller, more circumspect hug.

When had they started hugging him like this? Joe didn't remember exactly, but he knew it was after they'd started coming to Angelica's a couple of times a week.

"Yes, I am late, pumpkin." He kissed the top of Tori's head and ruffled Nick's hair.

"Your dinner's ready," Angelica called from the dining room. He stepped in to find the room readied for him as for a group of important guests—fresh flowers gracing the table and imparting a delightful scent to the whole room; a place set at the table's head complete with china and stemware; silver and a linen napkin, condiments, salt and pepper, all strategically arranged. As he watched, openmouthed with amazement, Angelica poured fresh lemonade over ice cubes in the goblet at his place.

"This is too much," he said, hesitating. "It's really too much."

"Come on, Daddy." Tori tugged on his hand. "You've gotta taste the mushroom quiche. I think it's even better than the spinach we had last week."

Conceding defeat, Joe sat. He closed his eyes and murmured a brief prayer, than tasted the mushroom quiche. As much as he'd prefer to find fault with it, he had to admit that it was every bit as wonderful as Tori had said.

"It's delicious," he decreed, suppressing a sigh while his children applauded his choice. *Everything about Angelica is delicious. And she makes it so easy, too easy. It will be difficult to keep my distance.*

* * *

It was Saturday and she hadn't seen Joe or his children since Wednesday evening when they'd eaten in her home. Not only that, but he'd already begged off for Monday, and she didn't know yet whether he'd be joining the group at the McAllister home on Sunday afternoon. Angelica pondered what a bold woman would do in this situation, and wasn't quite sure if she knew.

One thing she did know was that Tori and Nick would be playing soccer at the junior high school field this afternoon. Dare she show up uninvited? But other community members showed up from time to time, didn't they? And they weren't all invited. The school was public property, after all. What could anyone possibly say? Resolving to be there for the kids' game, she set about making a zucchini cake to share with everyone when the game was over. Maybe the way to a man's heart wasn't through his stomach; maybe it was through his children. Either way, the cake ought to work just as well.

"Dad, look who's here!" The kids were suiting up, putting on shin guards and pulling their long socks up over them, getting ready to go onto the field, when Nick made his announcement.

Joe looked up to find Angelica walking toward them. His heart leaped. *It should be sinking*, he thought grimly. *I should be worrying about how I'm going to let this woman down gently when she won't take subtle hints. Instead here I am with my heart racing, hoping she'll come over and stand next to me.*

She didn't. Instead she stopped demurely—rather coyly, he thought—next to the Duncans, whose two sons were playing in this game. "Mrs. Duncan," she said pleasantly. "I didn't realize your boys were playing with this group."

"They weren't until last week," Irene Duncan answered, and began a chatty discussion of how her son Jeremy had taken a call from Donny Phillips, who had played the first week after young Danny Sherwood had invited him.

"The game is really growing, isn't it?" Angelica said.

Irene quickly agreed. "We have enough players for three teams now," she told Angelica, "and it wouldn't take many more to make four."

"Maybe we need to look into creating a real league," Angelica said.

Irene purred, "Angelica, that would be wonderful."

A soccer league? Just like the kids had in Orange County? Joe wouldn't have believed it possible, but it looked like Angelica was on the verge of finding a way to make it happen. He wasn't sure how she did it, but she seemed to have a knack for making all kinds of things happen—like getting him to pray again, or having his children help with chores; like getting his children to hug him when he came in. *Like getting me to care about her, whether I want to or not.*

Joe dropped his jaw, surprised at himself. *Where did that thought come from?* Yet even as he tried to deny it, he knew in his heart it was true. He didn't love Angelica—not like he'd loved Roberta—and he knew it was not possible for him to care in that way. But care he did. The way he'd felt when he saw her coming toward him today proved that, if nothing else did.

He left his spot at the fifty-yard line and walked down to stand next to Angelica. "Hi," he said.

"Hi," she answered. She lit the whole playing field

with one of those brilliant sunrise smiles of hers, and his heartbeat shifted into overdrive. He stepped still closer, and put his hand in the small of her back. They were in public, and he thought she might draw away, but she leaned closer to him instead, smiling in a way that let Irene Duncan, or anyone else who was watching, know she was with Joe Vanetti, and proud of it.

He turned toward Irene Duncan, whom he knew to be one of the town's best "newscasters," and grinned at her speculative look. *Joe Vanetti,* he asked himself, *are you sure you know what you're doing? By the time you go to church tomorrow, everyone in Rainbow Rock will know you're dating Angelica DeForest.*

So? he answered his own speculation. *Let them know. It's true, isn't it?*

But he didn't want it to be true, did it? Wasn't he still trying to distance from her? What about his commitment to be fair?

You're thinking too hard, he decided finally. *She's here, you're here. . . . You might as well be here to-gether. You can still stand her up on Monday, just as you'd planned.* Later that evening, when he was alone, he could feel downright foolish. Later he could kick himself for letting Irene Duncan see him with Angelica. Later he could promise himself he'd stay away from her at church, making everyone disbelieve the rumor mills. Later.

Taking small solace in that thought, he drew Angelica closer.

Chapter Eight

Sunday, and everything remained as it had always been. Angelica still sat alone. Three rows forward and to the right, Joe sat with Max and Cretia and their combined offspring, forming the other adult bookend on the row of children. Though Angelica saw a few heads turn to look from her to Joe, though she heard a few mumbled speculations when she walked by, the rumors went nowhere. Worse, Joe remained distant and aloof. This week, he didn't even turn to look at her as he had so often in the past.

He looks haggard, she thought, amazed at how much his distress hurt her. *But maybe that's how it feels when you love someone. Maybe when you're in love, you hurt more for him than for yourself.* She couldn't say for certain—she was fairly new at love, after all—but that's how she felt when she looked at Joe. She only wished she could go to him, touch him, soothe away whatever was causing the deep wrinkles in his brow, the tension in his strong, bunched shoulders, the weariness in his eyes.

What would happen if I did go to him? she wondered, but even her new boldness quailed at the prospect of Joe's rejection. Perhaps it was better to wonder than to face the bitterness that would come with that kind of hurt. *But you already know, don't you?* She couldn't deny it. Joe was rejecting her now. For whatever reason, for whatever cause she didn't know about or fully understand, he was deliberately drawing away from her, purposefully distancing. It was almost too much to bear.

Then why . . . ? But there wasn't any point in wondering. Since that moment in the canyon when she'd opened her heart too much, revealed too much, and very nearly said too much, he'd been pulling away from her. Yes, there were moments when he seemed almost to be hers, when he pulled her closer or held her tighter. Lately all of them were moments she herself had arranged, whether wangling an invitation to the canyon and the fireworks, or inviting herself to his children's soccer game. Joe wanted to be close to her. He felt drawn to her on some levels. Still, when he was doing the thinking and planning, he pulled back farther, and farther still.

What to do? That was her question. Did the new, bold Angelica go for it? Did she fight for her man, using whatever means she had, fair or foul, to bring her to him? Or did she love him enough to let him go? She didn't know, but she knew she'd have to make a decision soon.

A future alone, without Joe near, stretched before her like a life sentence, so dim and heartless that she paled at the image. But a future with Joe when he didn't want her? That would even be worse.

Loving isn't easy, is it? her own thoughts teased her. Then she thought of the wonderful times when he had drawn toward her, of the magical moment in the canyon when he had kissed her like a starved man taking nurture from her lips, of the gentle moments when he had bowed his head at her dinner table and had prayed from his heart. *No*, she answered, *it's not easy. But it's worth it. It's worth whatever it costs.*

Joe wasn't going to the traditional McAllister family Sunday potluck. He wasn't. It would be too easy in the middle of all those couples to get paired off with Angelica, to have people thinking they belonged together, especially after the fireworks last week when they'd looked every inch the couple. He'd already planned to grill hamburger patties for Tori and Nick and a rib-eye steak for himself—*hah! So much for meatless meals!*— and he'd even bought ketchup and pickles and hamburger buns, plus some potato chips to round things out. He could cook for his own children, and he would, too.

When Sarah approached him after church to make sure he knew what time they were meeting and how to get there, he carefully explained that he had other plans. When Chris stopped to ask if he could take the kids out in his truck to give Joe some extra preparation time, he again carefully explained he didn't think they could make it today. When Meg said she was bringing her famous raw apple cake because she remembered how much Joe had liked it when they were kids, and Jim said he was hoping Joe was in good voice because they were looking forward singing with him, and Kurt said he was going to get some videotape of the kids playing together, and Alexa asked if she could interview Tori for a script she was working on while the kids were at the farm this afternoon, and Max said he was hoping they'd all ride with him, he *still* told them all that he had other plans. It was only when Cretia announced in front of Nick and Tori that she'd made enough Swedish meatballs for all of them and the kids began to beg him to let them go with Max and Cretia to the potluck, even if Joe wasn't going himself, that he finally capitulated.

"Traitors," he mumbled as he watched his children climb into Max's van, but he couldn't really blame them for liking Angelica. *He* liked Angelica. Sighing, he drove toward his home, trying to think of something he could offer to the potluck, something that wouldn't embarrass him. That made him think of Angelica and what a fine cook she was, and that thought made him feel guilty all over again. It was wrong to want Angelica simply because she was convenient to have around.

It's time you faced it, Joe, he lectured himself. *Angelica is a good fit in your life*. At that moment, the fact that he didn't love her seemed almost irrelevant.

Angelica stopped in the dooryard of the McAllister farm and breathed a deep sigh. The invitation wasn't nearly so interesting when it came to her alone, and not to her *with* Joe and his children. The amount of food she'd brought would surely have sufficed for them all. A huge *chili relleno* casserole, still warm and oozing with chilies and cheese, sat in the backseat, and she'd brought both a tossed green salad, dressing on the side, and a fruit salad, brimming with fresh nectarines and berries from her own gardens. She opened the car door and lifted a salad bowl in each hand, thinking to come back for the casserole. No sooner had she stepped onto the porch than she was very nearly knocked flat by a medium-sized boy in a superhero cape who dashed by as if he were flying.

Another boy—young Danny Sherwood, maybe?— was right on his heels and behind him came . . . Could that have been Nick Vanetti who just flew by?

Joe's here? The thought lifted her spirits as nothing had in days.

"Nicholas Vanetti, you'd better come back here now!" a young voice called from the side porch. Tori followed immediately after her announcement, running almost as fast as her brother.

"Whoa, there!" Angelica, holding both salads over her head just in case, put out a foot to distract Victoria.

"Oh, hi, Angelica," the little girl spoke, then she hollered again, "Nick, come back here!"

"What did he do?" Angelica asked.

"It wasn't him. It was Tyler. But Nick laughed when he did it." Tori was blushing furiously.

Angelica struggled to remember all the introductions from Fourth of July night. *Tyler. That would be Joan and Bob's son, from Winslow.* "Just what did Tyler do?"

Tori's face flamed in anger. "He dropped a *lizard tail* down the front of my blouse."

"A lizard tail?" Angelica made an appropriate face. "Yuck!"

"That's what *I* said." She seemed to feel validated, now that Angelica had agreed with her.

"Did you get it out?"

"Yeah, but I practically had a fit, and those nasty boys just stood there watching and laughing at me—even my own brother!"

Angelica fought down a mutinous grin, trying to remember that the scene wasn't funny to Tori. *Well, it wouldn't have been funny to you when you were eleven, either, and you remember far too well to think differently.* "Boys can be like that sometimes," she said sagely.

Tori sighed, a world-weary woman of eleven years. "Are men always like that?" she asked in disdain. "Don't they ever grow up?"

Angelica thought of one very grown-up man who was still something of a little boy inside, unable to make up his mind about what he really wanted. "No," she answered, shaking her head, "they never really do."

"Pity," Tori said wisely.

"Indeed," Angelica answered. Then, "I guess you're just going to have to talk to your father about Nick."

"Can't. He's not here."

"Oh." Her heart began shriveling within her.

"He should be coming in a little while, though."

"Oh!" It revived just-like-that, picking up speed.

She gave Tori a sympathetic, long-suffering smile. "Good luck," she said as Tori stalked to the tire swing for a sulk. As she watched the child disappear, Angelica thought, *Oh, Tori, dear, you're making it entirely too easy for them.*

Ouch! The thought struck her as if she'd been poleaxed between the ears. She practically went down under its force. In her dizzying head, it was her Grandma Poppy's voice she heard saying, *Angelica, dear, you're making it far too easy for him.*

She was making it easy, wasn't she? Her new boldness had given Joe Vanetti every excuse to take advantage of her goodness without having to make any commitments. Any time he wanted dinner at her home, all he had to do was call. If he wanted a comfortable companion for dinner, he could just ask. And if he wanted kisses? *Putty in his hands*, Angelica thought, disgusted with herself. She remembered hearing Grandma Poppy tell her mother that a woman had to play hard to get. She'd always thought it foolishness. If two mature people liked each other, there was no point in silly games, now was there? Still, she knew from watching the boys try to outrun one another on the soccer field that a victory too easily won was also easily forgotten, or even discarded. *And isn't that exactly what Joe's doing now? Discarding you?*

She humphed, disgusted at herself. Maybe Grandma Poppy's Rules for Dating weren't quite so silly after all.

At a loss to decide what to take to the potluck—hamburgers wouldn't do, and there wasn't much else in the house—Joe finally chose to leave empty-handed. He rationalized there would probably be more than enough food, anyway: they could get by without his contribution. Already feeling trapped into this arrangement, he was in no mood to feel guilty about food as well.

Desultory and disgruntled, he climbed behind the wheel and headed for Rainbow Rock Farms. As he drove, he couldn't help noticing streaks of lightning crashing over the far peaks. An occasional rumble of thunder was loud enough to hear, even at this distance. *Looks like an afternoon thundershower,* he thought wearily. *Well, why not? It's not my day, anyway.*

He pulled into the dooryard of the McAllister home just in time to see Tori come flying out of the side yard, her tattletale voice going at full speed. "Dad, I've been waiting for you to get here. You should have seen what Nick did!" she began, and Joe sighed. It was going to be a miserable afternoon.

                        *   *   *

Angelica was having the time of her life, or so it appeared every time Joe looked at her. He'd never seen her so animated, or so comfortable in a social setting. The aloof teenager he'd known long ago had utterly vanished, replaced by a sleek, sophisticated beauty who seemed to know how to say all the right things to charm every man in the room, married though they were. She was even charming their wives! Worse still, she'd hardly seemed to notice when he came in, offering him nothing more than a brief, pleasant hello before moving on. *And you'd begun to think you were something special in her life,* he reminded himself grimly. *You'd even decided she might be falling in love with you. Halt! Small chance of that!*

If Angelica was in love, he wouldn't know it by looking at her now. She sat at the table relishing her food, between bites telling a story about a man who tried to take a subway train while carrying a bass violin; everyone was half hysterical with laughter. She was clearly playing to the crowd, just as she always had when hiding behind her viola, and she'd hardly seemed to notice he was there, except, perhaps, for the early moments after his arrival when he'd argued that Angelica had brought enough food for all of them and she had responded, "But that's my contribution, Joe. Where's yours?"

So he sat at the table at Meg and Sarah's sufferance, following Cretia's promise that she'd be sure her brother brought plenty of food next time, and listening as Angelica smiled and laughed and wormed her way into everyone's hearts. Everyone's. Even his. Especially his.

When the lightning crackled and the downpour began,

Joe was neither impressed nor depressed. He almost expected it.

"Glorious, isn't it?" Cretia said.

Joe couldn't disagree despite his mood. "Yeah," he said. "Beautiful."

They stood on the front porch of the McAllister home, gazing toward the eastern foothills where a magnificent double rainbow filled the sky. The rain had let up—at least, where they were—and most of their family and friends had walked toward the field so the farrowing barn wouldn't block their view. Kurt and Alexa had invited Angelica to go with them and she'd hurried away without even looking back at Joe. She hadn't so much as stood next to him all afternoon.

"You're sulking, you know." Cretia had never been one for mincing words.

"Mind your own business, sis."

"When it concerns my older brother, I think it *is* my business." Cretia's eyes twinkled. "She isn't paying you much attention today, is she?"

Joe's tone grew biting. "Like I said before—"

"I know, I know. Mind my own business." She sobered. "I had the impression you two were getting serious."

If Joe's tone had been biting before, it was downright threatening now. "Look, sis—"

"You can't shut me out, Joe, so you might as well talk to me. Besides, I have spies in the inner circle. Nick and Victoria both sing like canary birds." She adopted the dialect used in Chicago gangster movies.

Joe groaned. "So you want me to think I have to come

clean, sharing all the intimate details of my formerly personal life."

"You know, sarcasm is not your most attractive aspect."

"Sorry." He didn't seem sorry, and he didn't say more.

Cretia breathed deeply of the rain-laden air. "You know what the trouble with rainbows is?"

"Huh?" Joe furrowed his brow.

"The trouble with rainbows," she repeated airily.

"No, I guess I don't." He waited.

"You can't predict them." Cretia's eyes watched the bow of color in the sky. "We all know what causes them, and we can see the elements coming together and guess that maybe there'll be a rainbow soon, but nobody ever knows exactly when or where we'll see it."

Joe stared at his sister, wondering when she had lost her mind. She'd seemed fairly sane this morning.

"They're kind of like love, really," Cretia went on.

Joe groaned. She hadn't changed the subject at all.

"No, really. Think about it, Joe. We can see two attractive people coming together and think, 'Hmm. Maybe there'll be a match soon,' but no one ever knows for sure until it happens." This time her eyes were following Angelica, whose silvery laughter wafted toward them on the breeze. "We can never predict when love will come into our lives—either the first or the second time."

Joe had heard more than enough. "Suppose," he said, a sarcastic edge to his reasonable tone, "that you've found your own personal rainbow. Maybe you're one of the rare few who followed it to its end and found the pot of gold. You've found your gold and you've spent it. Now it's gone. End of story."

Cretia pointed to the place near the northern horizon where the rainbow appeared to originate, then traced its arch clear across the sky to the point in the south where it vanished. Her voice was hushed. "Every rainbow has two ends, you know."

Joe sneered. "You should have been a psychologist."

"Ooh, now you're being nasty." Cretia smiled, unperturbed.

"Or maybe a grief counselor. You'd be good at it." He put on a nasal falsetto: "I know you just lost the love of your life, Mr. Smith, but it's time to get over it and move on. Fifty dollars, please." He jabbed his hand into the air before her face.

The tight little muscle in Cretia's jaw told Joe she was struggling with her temper. "I was joking about you being nasty," she said, her voice low. "But you really can be unkind when you choose to."

Joe couldn't help feeling a little ashamed. "Okay, that one was uncalled for," he admitted, "but one thing I don't need is more platitudes about how I need to get on with living."

"I'm trying to avoid the platitudes, Joe, but you were a lost soul after Roberta died, and these last few weeks have brought back some of the spark and energy I remember in my brother. I have to be grateful for anyone or anything that can do that—either for you or the kids. If there's someone who can bring the joy back into life for all three of you—"

"Stop right there." The words were a warning. "I don't want to hear any more."

"Okay," Cretia agreed, though her acceptance was slow. "I won't say any more then. At least, not now. But think about it, Joe. You're right that few people get to keep the pot of gold. Fewer still get to keep it twice. It would be foolish to walk away from it, assuming it will always be there for the taking." She flashed another look toward Angelica, then patted his arm as she left.

Joe hadn't intended to "think about it," but he couldn't seem to stop himself. She was right. Cretia was right. A woman like Angelica wouldn't always be there for the taking. She hadn't been there for him today, not as he had wished her to be. Maybe he was going to have to consider exactly what she meant in his life, and whether it would be better to offer her a union built on fondness and attraction—even if he couldn't offer love—than to let her walk out of his life. The idea certainly had appeal.

The rainbow's brilliant colors began to fade and the extended McAllister family turned back toward the farmhouse. Angelica kept her gaze riveted on the front door, watching Joe only from the corner of her eye. She made a point of laughing merrily at a quip from one of the children. Inside she was pleading, *Notice me, Joe. Please notice me.* She all but sighed. She'd played this part of the game before, and struggling to be noticed was exhausting. The game Grandma Poppy's rules dictated was a risky business, with winners or losers and no option of coming in second. She longed to just take Joe into her arms and talk some sense into him, but she sensed that particular form of honesty would work against her just now.

Let him make up his own mind, she decided. *Then, if he wants me, I can be free to tell him how all this play-acting and posturing felt for me.* And if he didn't? Well, at least she'd know she'd given it her all.

Sarah announced it was time for dessert, and the various guests all found places at the two huge tables Chris had set up in the great room. Sarah brought out small plates and forks, Meg and Alexa set on the dessert dishes people had brought, and Angelica joined in, helping serve up portions to order. When everyone was busy eating again, Chris spoke. "You know, I saw the end of the kids' soccer game yesterday. I was really impressed. I had no idea so many kids were showing up now, and some of them were really getting good. They're developing sound skills."

Angelica saw an opportunity. "You know, I think with a little effort, we could easily have a youth soccer league in town by this fall."

Everyone turned to look at her as if the idea had never occurred to them before and was taking a moment to sink in. "What would you need?" Chris asked.

"Well, first of all, someone to organize it," she answered.

"That would be you, of course," Kurt said. "You've been great so far."

Angelica felt her throat tightening. Her? Running a soccer league? Then inspiration, or perhaps desperation, stepped in to save her. "I was thinking of Irene Duncan," she said coolly, though Irene's name had only occurred to her at that moment. "She has two boys playing right now, and I understand there's a sister who might like to play, too. She's the one who thought we could get four full teams going by this fall."

"Four?" Meg was wide-eyed. "I had no idea you had that many kids turning up."

Joe nodded. "We had thirty-six on Saturday."

"Whew!" Meg blew out a long, slow whistle. "Then

with a little advance advertising, you could probably manage six teams, maybe more."

"Maybe," Joe said. "If we could afford the advertising."

Chris chimed in. "The farm has been doing well this year, and we could probably use the tax write-off." He looked toward Sarah. "I think we could afford the price of some flyers to hand around at school, and the local radio station would probably do public service announcements for free."

Sarah nodded agreement. "I think we could manage that, and we know other people who are in business locally. Some of them might be willing to help with administrative costs, in exchange for advertising, of course."

"Of course." Angelica's answer was smooth. "Uniforms would be another big cost. We wouldn't need anything fancy, but the kids ought at least to have matching jerseys, just so they can always tell which moving shapes are on which team."

"Good point." It was Kurt, speaking up for the first time. "I'd have to speak with my partner, you understand—" He looked toward Meg. "—but I think Rainbow Productions could probably front the funds for a few jerseys, enough for six teams, anyway. What do you think, partner?"

"No doubt about it," Meg answered firmly. "Consider it done. You get a league going, we'll put up the cost of jerseys to outfit six teams."

"Great!" Angelica looked impressed. "We'd have to make sure the schools didn't mind us using their fields—"

"No problem." It was Sarah speaking. "My friend

Eden Redhorse wasn't able to join us today, but she just got elected to next year's school board. As long as you organize the league for the fall season, so you're not interfering with intramural play, I'm sure you can get approval."

"And the goal boxes and nets?" Angelica said. "Do you think they'd let us use the equipment at the school?"

"I doubt that." Jim, who had been listening quietly while playing with his young daughter, now spoke quietly. "It wouldn't serve the schools' purposes to let someone else use, and possibly damage, their equipment. But I know a local art dealer who could probably front the cash for a couple of goal boxes, at least for official league play."

Kurt patted his older brother on the back. "Thanks, Jim. I was wondering when you were going to climb on board."

To Angelica's gratification, the next few minutes went exactly that way. She'd been right to identify these people as the movers and shakers of Rainbow Rock. When the McAllisters and their extended friends and family got together, she guessed they could move mountains. They could surely create a soccer league. In a half hour this Sunday afternoon, they'd almost done it, complete with a setup for phone trees, volunteer coaches, and a committee to form a list of players' rules.

A short while later she sat on the porch swing of the McAllister home, feeling rather pleased with what they'd accomplished.

"Gloating?" Joe asked.

Angelica turned with a gasp, both startled and hurt by the negative tone of Joe's comment, though she refused to let him know it. "Pleased," she answered, regaining composure. "It looks like the kids may have their soccer league after all."

"If they do, they'll have you to thank for it." Joe sat down beside her, possessively taking her hand. She quietly drew it away. He scowled, but went on with his comment. "What you did in there was really quite remarkable."

Though his tone had been admiring, it had also been grudging. She shrugged it off. "It was nothing. I just turned the idea over to capable people who knew what they were doing. They did the rest."

"You handled it splendidly," Joe said. He seemed not to know quite what to do with his hands, and so ended up folding them in front of him. "You seem to have a real knack for organizing people."

"That's funny," Angelica said. "I don't have much experience with it. I was always so afraid of people."

"I could never tell." There seemed to be an accusative edge in his voice. "You performed in public so often."

"That was different." Angelica forced herself to relax against the back of the bench. She didn't know why Joe was being nasty, but she didn't like it one bit, though she refused to give him the satisfaction of knowing he'd hurt her. "I always felt it was the viola they were watching, that I was sort of an appendage to the instrument."

"That *is* funny," Joe said, and the edge in the comment was so sharp it made Angelica want to get up and run. She didn't, but waited patiently for what came next. When it came, it was so pleasant, so smoothly delivered, that it shocked her. "The kids and I have had a change of schedule," he said, oh so coolly. "Turns out we'll be able to come to dinner tomorrow after all."

Because Angelica had looked away just before Joe

spoke, she had the luxury of closing her eyes and breathing in slowly before turning back to him, a look of pure sweetness on her countenance. "I'm sorry, Joe, but when you said you couldn't make it, I made other plans." *It's not a lie*, she reasoned quickly. *I have the letter I've been planning to write to my cousin, Heidi, and I really do need to wash my hair. . . .* "Maybe some other time." She stood, smiling dismissively.

"Yeah, yeah, sure," Joe said, staring after her as if she'd just dropped a live grenade in his lap.

A few minutes later, he rounded up his children and headed for home. When Tori asked, "What's wrong, Dad?," he growled, "Not a thing, Victoria," but he couldn't help feeling as if someone had reached inside him and stirred hard.

Chapter Nine

Joe spent a miserable Monday without Angelica. That evening was even worse. A half-dozen times he considered picking up the phone to see if she really did have other plans, but his pride kept his actions in check. All day Tuesday he thought about the next afternoon when he took Tori to her lesson. He was all smiles when the lesson concluded and he asked Angelica to join them for dinner. She was equally smiley in rejecting the invitation, citing "other plans." Thinking he'd get a headstart on the weekend, he asked her to join them for Friday night. Still smiling sweetly, she told him her cousin was probably coming to visit and she'd be busy all weekend, though Joe could call Thursday to double-check, if he wished. Joe was practically seething by the time he left Angelica's. The effect was not lost on his daughter.

"Dad, what's wrong?" Tori demanded as they pulled away.

"Nothing, pumpkin." Joe kept his eyes on the road.

"Don't pretend with me, Dad."

Joe couldn't help reflecting that in that moment, Tori sounded a lot like her mother. "I'm not pretending, honey. Really, everything's okay."

"So if everything's so okay, how come we never see Angelica anymore?"

Joe let out a long, frustrated sigh. "I don't know, honey."

Victoria narrowed her eyes. "Did you do something to hurt her feelings? 'Cause if you did, Nick and I are both gonna be real mad."

Joe didn't know whether to laugh or cry. He licked his lips and looked his daughter in the eye. "No, honey. At least, I don't think I did."

"Then why doesn't she ever want to see us?"

Joe could only shrug. He was wondering that himself.

Tori sighed. "I thought maybe she was going to be our new stepmother."

"What?" He jerked the wheel. If there'd been a full-grown elephant in the road, he surely would have hit it. He swallowed as he brought the car under control. "What did you say?"

Tori straightened. She sounded so serious when she answered. "Nick and me, we've been talking about it. We thought maybe you were going to ask Angelica to marry you. Then she'd be our new stepmother."

"You thought that, huh?" *When did my children start doing all this thinking?*

"Well, yeah. I mean, for a while there, you were inviting her out with us all the time, and we were coming to her place a lot, and she was teaching Nick and me how to work in the garden and how to play computer games and stuff. . . ." Tori turned her face toward the window. "It just kinda seemed like what you'd do if you were trying to find us a good mom."

Good mom? Joe shivered. *I ought to leave that one alone.* But he couldn't. He'd thought too little about how all this was affecting his children. "So you two thought Angelica would be a good stepmother."

"Well, yeah." She turned back to face her father. "We really like her, Dad. Then after a couple of times when we saw you kissing her—"

Joe felt his face grow warm. "You saw us—"

Tori clucked her tongue. "It's not exactly like you were hiding. You kissed her on the porch swing, and in the park, and that day in the canyon—"

"Okay, okay. I get the message." *And all that time I thought I was being discreet.*

"Anyway, it seemed to us like you probably liked her, too." She pinned her father with a look. "So what are you going to do about it?"

Tori was pushing, and Joe was seeing a new, more adult side of his daughter. "You think I ought to do something?"

"Duh. Yeah, I do. Nick does, too. Get her to go out with you again. Maybe ask her out sometime when Nick and I aren't around. You know, just the two of you. Women like that."

"They do, huh?" He didn't know whether to be annoyed or amused.

"Well, yeah. I mean, I would if I were all grown up. You at least ought to try it. Maybe you can still talk her into getting married." Joe was at the point of asking *What if I don't want to get married?* when Tori's eyes narrowed. "Don't blow it, Dad. We might not get a chance like this again."

Stifling a chuckle, Joe drove his daughter home.

"So anyway, that's what Tori thinks." Joe had been distressed enough by the talk in the car that he'd just repeated it all to his sister while Nick and Victoria played computer games with their cousins and he worked in the kitchen helping Max and Cretia clean up, which seemed like the least he could do after inviting himself and his kids to dinner. Max had wisely found an excuse to disappear as soon as Joe said he wanted to talk.

"Sounds like sage advice to me." Cretia nodded. "Tori's smart."

"Sage advice? From an eleven-year-old?"

"Out of the mouths of babes," Cretia quoted. "As I recall, I was just saying something similar myself, although I was trying to reach you with silly rainbow analogies at the time." She gave him a narrowed look, and for a moment, she looked a lot like Tori.

Or maybe that look is born in the XX chromosomes? Joe wondered. *It seems to be in every woman's repertoire.*

"Maybe poetry is over your head," Cretia continued. "Maybe what you need is more akin to a knock upside the ears with a blunt instrument." She took his face in her hands, leaned toward him, and spoke loudly, enunciating each word, "MAR-RY HER, JOE! Catch her before she gets away."

Then Joe said aloud what he'd said only to himself. "I've thought about it." He saw Cretia's surprised expression. "I have, a lot. I mean, she's good for the kids—"

"And for you."

"And for me, too," he admitted, "but I've been afraid it wouldn't be fair. To her, I mean."

Cretia's look changed. Her brows pulled together. She reached for a chair and motioned him into one. "Not fair? In what way?"

Digging deeply into his emotions was difficult for Joe. Sharing them was something he rarely did. He took a deep breath and swallowed hard, pulled out a chair across from Cretia's and sat down, fumbled a little with things on the table. . . .

"In what way would it not be fair?" Cretia demanded.

Joe knew he needed to answer. "I mean," he began, wondering exactly what he did mean, "that it wouldn't be fair to ask her to love me when I'm not in love with her."

Cretia laughed aloud—laughed so hard, in fact, that she had to wipe her eyes before she could get control again. "You could have fooled me," she said, her voice ripe with meaning. "For the last several weeks you've acted like a man very much in love, even besotted with it."

"I have?" Joe cocked a brow.

"You most definitely have."

He sighed. "I think you're confusing attraction with something more meaningful."

"Attraction? You think that's all you feel?"

"Well, I'm fond of her, too. I like her a lot, actually. And I admire her. She's much more accomplished than I'd ever imagined, in a variety of ways. I respect her. I enjoy being around her. . . ." He paused.

"And that's not love?" Cretia was giving him that

cool, clear look that told him she was reading right through him.

He sighed. "I used to think so. But I've been in love now—really, deeply, truly in love. I know what it feels like, and I just don't feel—"

"Hold it." Cretia put out her hand. "Are you telling me that you're pulling away from Angelica because you don't feel the same way about her that you felt about Roberta?"

"Well, yeah. I don't think I can ever love again the way I loved Roberta. And it just doesn't feel right to—"

Cretia harrumphed in disgust. "You really are a fool, you know that?"

"Huh?" Joe wondered when he'd lost the thread of this conversation.

"Talk to me again when you and Angelica have been married for fourteen years and have raised a couple of kids together. *Of course* you don't feel the same way!"

Joe swallowed. "Huh?" he said again.

"Joe, what's unfair is comparing the way you felt about the love of your youth and the mother of your children to the way you feel about someone you've known only a few weeks." She bit her lip. "Listen. On the day you married Roberta, you thought you loved her more than it was possible for any man to love a woman, right?"

"Well, yeah."

"And then, when Tori was born, you found you loved your wife ever so much more than you had on the day you married her. Am I right?"

Joe nodded. "Yeah. So?"

"So if you want a fair comparison, think of the way

you felt about Roberta when you'd only been dating her a few weeks. If you feel that strongly about Angelica, or even close, you know you're on the way to finding the gold at the end of the rainbow all over again."

"Oh." Joe blinked several times. He swallowed. "Oh."

"I can see the light is finally dawning." Her voice rang with sarcasm.

"I really am in love with Angelica," Joe said, his voice filled with wonder. "I'm in love with Angelica!"

Cretia sighed. "Took you long enough."

Then Joe sighed. "Maybe too long. She doesn't want to see me."

"Who says?"

"Well, *she* does. At least, she always has an excuse not to see me, every time I ask."

"And just how are you asking?"

So Joe told his sister about the conversation at Angelica's house that afternoon.

Cretia shook her head. "Ah, men. She wants to be courted, Joe. She deserves that. She doesn't just want you to invite yourself and your kids over to eat. She wants you to spend time with her without the kids in tow. She wants you to spend a little effort wooing her, telling her you like and admire and respect her, telling her you love her. Think about it: Would you ever have courted Roberta by asking her to baby-sit?"

"Ouch. Somebody take that knife out of my back, please."

"You deserve it," Cretia said calmly. "And you know I'm only saying it for your own good."

"One of those this-hurts-me-more-than-it-hurts-you kind of things?"

"Well, no, actually. It hurts you a lot more than it hurts me, but it's good for you, anyway."

Joe nodded. "Oh, I see."

"So what are you going to do about it?"

"Tori just asked me the same thing."

"And?"

"I'm not sure."

"Better think of something soon, big brother. You don't wanta blow this one."

"Tori said that, too."

Cretia pushed her chair back and stood. "As I was saying, that daughter of yours is a smart young lady."

It was Thursday afternoon and Angelica worked in her garden, discussing her problems with the vegetables. "I thought he cared enough to try a little harder," she told the green beans as she made her way between rows, carefully plucking their fruit. "I hoped he'd get frustrated if he had to work to see me," she reported to the beets as she thinned them, keeping the small bulbs for her dinner. "I thought hard-to-get was a good idea, but do you think I'm overdoing it?" she asked the eggplants, whose blossoms nodded sagely in the breeze.

All she knew for sure was, she was miserable. If Joe didn't break down soon, she was at risk of running to him, begging him to take her in as his cook or governess or cleaning lady, or anything that would allow her to be close to him. *And to the kids*, she added, thinking of how much life they'd brought into this tired old-people's house.

She carried her produce into the kitchen and began preparing a simple meal. *Funny*, she thought. *Eating alone never bothered me before*. She'd cook the tiny beets she'd pulled, and steam the green beans. Then she'd tear up some salad greens from this morning's picking. . . . She reached into the refrigerator for the poppyseed dressing—Nick's Grandma Poppy dressing—and a sob caught in her throat. She sank down in front of her open refrigerator and sat on the cold tile floor as the tears gathered in her eyes and trickled down her cheeks. She missed Nick. She missed Tori. She missed Joe so much she could hardly think of anything else. "What am I going to do?" she asked the vegetables that stared at her from the shelves.

That was when her front doorbell rang. *I'm not expecting anyone.* She caught her reflection in the stainless steel bowl that held her salad greens. *Goodness! Whoever it is, I don't want them seeing me like this!*

"Just a minute!" she called to the door. "I'll be right there."

She stood. Feeling foolish, she shut the refrigerator and hurried to the kitchen sink, ran some water to rinse her face and dried it on the dish towel nearby, brushed bits of dirt and vegetable matter from her gardening shorts and T-shirt, then hurried to the front entrance, pulling her hair out of its ponytail and shaking it loose as she went. She opened the door and looked out, expecting to see a Girl Scout or a kid selling magazines. "Joe!"

" 'Evening, Angelica. Here, these are for you."

She stood looking at them. "Flowers? For me?"

"I know you grow your own," he said, still holding the flowers out in front of him, "but there were varieties in this bouquet that I'd never seen in your house or yard and they smelled nice. I just thought . . ."

For a long moment, Angelica stared at him. Then she shook herself into motion. "I'm sorry. Here. Please come in." She opened the screen and took the flowers. "I'll find a vase for these." As she walked toward the kitchen, she remembered her manners. "Have a seat if you like. I'll just be a minute."

"No hurry," Joe said, and sat on the red velvet love seat.

He looks wonderful! I don't think I've ever seen him look more wonderful. She hurried to get a vase, a nice one. *His hair is still damp, and he looks freshly shaved. He must have stopped at home to clean up before he came over. I wonder why. Just for me? And flowers! What's that all about? Could it be playing hard-to-get is working? And I look so awful.* She stuck her head into the half bath next to the kitchen and grimaced at her reflection. *Oh, well, nothing to be done about it now.* Putting a little water in the bottom of her cut-crystal vase, she returned to the living room with Joe's flowers.

"Thank you," she said belatedly. "They're lovely." She put the flowers on the music table and sat in an overstuffed chair nearby. She tried to keep her voice cool as she asked, "To what do I owe this visit?"

"It's Thursday," he said, and she waited. "You said I should check on Thursday to see whether or not your cousin was coming."

"Oh, yes." She'd almost forgotten the fiction about her cousin. "As it turns out, they're going to wait for me to visit them later in the summer."

"Ah," Joe said. "That two-week hiatus you mentioned when Tori first started her lessons."

"Yes." Angelica remembered that conversation. It seemed to have happened a long time ago. *So much has happened since then. . . .*

"Does that mean you're free for dinner tomorrow?"

Should I tell him I have other plans? No, enough of that! Besides, he even brought flowers. "Yes," she said, hoping to win him with her smile. "Were you thinking of our usual Friday night dinner?"

"No," he said.

"No?"

"I've asked Cretia to keep the kids tomorrow evening. With your permission, I'd like to take you out. Just the two of us, alone."

"Oh." Angelica stood. "Joe, are you asking me for a date?"

Joe stood, too, and took a step toward her. "Yeah, I am. Do you mind?"

She giggled, then hiccuped, fighting down the impulse to throw herself into his arms. "I think it's very . . . sweet."

He stepped closer. "Angelica . . ."

Whether he leaped into her arms, or she into his, the effect was the same. One long, long kiss later, he pulled his lips away from hers, touching them instead to her cheeks and forehead. "I've missed you," he murmured between kisses.

"I've missed you, too," she said, eagerly turning her face up to receive more.

Joe straightened, though he kept his arms around her. "What time tomorrow?"

As soon as you can be here. Sooner! "Does six sound okay?"

He stroked her upper arms. "Six will be fine." For a long moment, they studied one another. "Um, I guess I'd better be going."

"I'll walk you to the door."

Arms around one another, they slowly strolled to the

front entrance. Angelica let him go as he dipped his head to take her lips again. "Tomorrow," he said.

"Tomorrow." She watched until his car disappeared at the top of her street. Then she jumped into the air and screamed, "Yes!"

Joe drove away from Angelica's home feeling happier than he had in months. *Thank goodness Cretia is smarter about these things than I am.* He made a mental note to buy her some flowers, too. He thought of Angelica as she'd looked when she opened her door. *She must have come in fresh from the garden,* he thought. *The smell of the earth and the flowers was still ripe on her skin, and in her hair.* Thinking now of that velvety skin and silken hair, he longed to kiss her, to hold her again.

Thanks to Cretia he finally understood that the lure to hold Angelica was more than mere physical attraction. In his entire life, he'd felt this way about two women. He'd married the first one. Now, if the fates were good to him, he was going to marry the second. *There's only one thing more I have to do first,* he declared to himself. Instead of driving toward his sister's house, he took the short drive into the bluffs overlooking Rainbow Rock, stopped his car, and sat still, watching the shadows lengthen in the bowl-shaped valley as the sun sank low behind him.

Joe closed his eyes. It took him a while to summon the face and form of his first wife. "Roberta," he whispered, eyes closed. "Roberta." Then she was there—at least, in his imagination. He'd talked to her this way many times since her death, since she'd left him, though never if there was anyone else around to hear. He wasn't crazy. He knew he wasn't, but loneliness did crazy things to a man. He sighed.

"I'm here, Joe," the image of Roberta said to him, and he knew he was ready.

"I've missed you."

The image smiled. "I've missed you, too."

She looked lovely. When he conjured her up like this, she almost always looked just as he'd last seen her alive, just as she'd looked before she drove out to go to work that last morning. For a moment, he admired her: her petite size-eight figure, her shining auburn hair wrapped neatly on the back of her head, her professional dress suit and navy pumps, her dark navy-blue eyes and flawless skin. She had always been beautiful. "You look beautiful," he said.

"I look the way you want me to look," Roberta's image answered. She had always been sensible, too.

"I'm thinking of getting married again," he said. *No point in beating around the bush.*

"Oh? Who is she?"

"A woman I knew in high school. Since junior high, really. I mean, I've known her since we were kids, but I've only really started getting to know her just lately, just since I brought the kids back to Rainbow Rock."

"And you love her?" The Roberta image smiled, not a hint of jealousy in her voice.

"Yes," he said, "I do. Not like I loved you. No mortal being could have loved you more than I did—"

"I know, Joe. I know." The image of Roberta leaned toward him. He could almost feel her touch, and he ached for it. "But you do love her?"

"Yes, I do. I'm sorry. I didn't want to fall in love again. I just . . . I hope you don't mind, too much."

"Oh, Joe." She laughed, the deep, throaty laughed he remembered so well. "Of course I don't mind. You didn't think I'd want you to spend the rest of your life alone, did you?"

He hadn't expected that. "I . . . I guess I hadn't thought about it."

She sat back and crossed her legs. "Then maybe it's time you did."

"You wouldn't mind if I got married again?" Joe couldn't keep the surprise out of his voice.

"Oh, Joe." She laughed again, and he remembered so many things he had loved about her. "Joseph, Joseph . . ." Finally she said, "It wasn't my idea to die. You know that, don't you?"

A familiar lump rose in his throat, that lump he always got whenever he thought of Roberta's death. "I know."

"If I could still be there with you, that's the only place I'd want to be." The image of Roberta leaned toward him yearningly. "But just because I can't be with you, that doesn't mean I want you to die, too, or to live like a monk, either."

He could barely choke out an answer. "No?"

"No." Warmth filled Roberta's smile. "Oh, Joe, my love. You're a healthy man in his prime. You need a woman to love, someone warm and caring who will love you in return, someone you can hold in the night and talk with in the day. . . . And then there are our children to think about."

"Our children?"

"Yes, Joseph, our children. Victoria is reaching the age when she'll need a mother to show her what it means to be a woman. Nicholas will soon be discovering that girls are different from boys and wanting to talk with his mother about some of the peculiar things the female of the species does. . . . I hope the woman you've found is good with children."

"She's wonderful," Joe answered, thinking of Angelica. The image of Roberta flickered faintly, and he brought his full attention back. "Both kids . . . that is, both children really like her a lot."

"Then I approve," the Roberta image said.

"You do?"

"Most definitely. And may I wish you both all the happiness in the world." She stood. "You know, don't you, that I won't be able to come to you like this after you've taken another wife?"

Joe frowned. "I guess I hadn't realized."

"It's all right," she said. "It's time for you to let me go."

He swallowed. "You won't mind?"

The image breathed deeply. "Maybe a little. I'll try not to." Already she was beginning to flicker, and he knew she was slipping away.

"I love you." He reached toward her.

"And I love you," she answered. "I always will."

Then she was gone, and Joe was alone. He looked around, wondering when it had grown dark. Then he said a soft good-bye to the memory of his late wife, and drove toward the Carmody house and his waiting children.

In the days that followed, Joe courted Angelica as ardently as any man had ever courted a woman. On Friday he brought her candy, then took her out for Thai food. On Saturday they went to the kids' soccer game, then took a picnic—one Joe himself had prepared—to the park. On Sunday he asked her to join the family in church, then sat smiling at Irene Duncan with one arm around his daughter and the other around the woman he hoped to marry. Though they were invited to join the McAllisters again, he opted to ask Angelica to his home instead where he cooked for the family, carefully serving fresh pasta primavera with salad and vegetables from Angelica's garden.

On Monday she asked them all to her house again, then on Tuesday they went out for pizza, and so it went. For the rest of the month of July there wasn't a day when they didn't see each other. Many times they spent the whole day together, and their days often lasted into the evening.

But the month was winding down, and soon the time came when Angelica would be leaving to visit her cousin Heidi.

"I'll miss you," Joe told her as they waited in the Holbrook Municipal Airport.

"I'll miss you, too," she said, "but it's only two weeks, and you can always call me."

"Two weeks seems like a long time," Joe answered. Then a thought seemed to occur to him. "Phoenix isn't that far away. Maybe the kids and I will come down for a visit."

Angelica shook her head. "Don't be silly, Joe. You're new in this job and I'm sure you don't have any vacation time yet. Besides, we've practically lived together in recent days. You can probably use a break."

"I don't want a break." Joe's voice sounded peevish. "I like being with you all the time."

"I'll be back," Angelica promised as her flight was called.

Joe kissed her good-bye—a long, hungry kiss that

made her wish she wasn't leaving—and Angelica hurried toward her plane. But as she climbed aboard and turned to wave toward the terminal, she couldn't help thinking that Joe still hadn't declared himself, and she still had no idea where their relationship was going.

Chapter Ten

Heidi Lunsford Smith was the youngest child of the youngest brother of Rowena Lunsford DeForest, Angelica's mother. That meant she was only a couple of years older than Angelica and, in both age and emotion, the closest family Angelica had left. The two girls had been friends during their teenaged years and had remained close confidantes throughout their early adulthood as well. That was why, on this sizzling evening in the second week of August, Heidi was willing to tolerate the tension that seemed to ooze from Angelica's every pore.

"Quit pacing, will you?" Heidi said, though not unkindly.

"I can't help it." Angelica sat, but almost immediately began pacing again. "I keep thinking Joe is going to call."

"Of course Joe is going to call." Heidi used her exasperated tone. "He's called every evening since you got here, plus twice last Saturday."

Angelica stood still for a moment, tapping her foot, then immediately resumed pacing. "I just wish I knew it meant something."

Heidi, who by now had heard the story of everything Joe Vanetti had ever said or done since Angelica was in seventh grade, quipped wryly, "I know one thing it will mean for sure."

"And that is?"

"Your friend Joe is going to have one heckuva phone bill."

"Yuck-yuck. Very funny." Angelica scowled, then sprang at the phone as it rang. "Hello?" She handed the receiver to her cousin. "For you."

"*Every* call can't be Joe." Heidi took the phone.

Heidi's call ended quickly. As she hung up, she said to Angelica, "You know, it probably wouldn't hurt for you to call him one night."

"Do you think? I haven't much experience with the etiquette of such things, and I don't want to seem overeager."

"Dear one . . ." Heidi paused to pat her hand in sympathy. "At this stage, you need to seem a little eager. You don't want him to think he can draw this dating stuff out forever."

"Oh, Heidi, if I only knew for sure . . ." But her comment was interrupted by another phone call, and this one was Joe.

Some time later, Angelica resurfaced into the real world to find Heidi relaxing in the kitchen with her husband, James, while their teenagers played in the pool outside. She went to join the adults in the kitchen.

"So that was the incomparable but slow-moving Joe?" James teased.

Angelica made a face at James, then spoke to Heidi. "I wish I understood what's going on with him. First he can hardly stay away, but it almost feels like he's taking advantage of a convenience. Then he has too much going on to see me. Then when I claim I have too much going on to see him, he suddenly acts like an ardent suitor, only he never talks about any kind of future. I don't understand it at all. Sometimes I feel like I don't understand *him* at all."

"We men are really pretty easy to understand. Just see that all our basic appetites are met and give us the remote control." James shrugged.

"I wish it were so easy." Angelica pouted.

"I'm no expert," Heidi began tentatively, and both James and Angelica turned to listen, "but it seems to me that your Joe is just having a little trouble making up his mind."

Angelica wrinkled her nose. "I already *know* that part."

"But there is a logical explanation for it, if you think of it in just the right way."

"And that would be?"

"Picture a married man, a family man like our James here." She playfully patted her husband's cheek and he offered a saintly pose. "He adores his children and is absolutely devoted to his wife."

"Okay. So far, so good." Angelica finally sat, concentrating on the picture Heidi painted with her words.

"Beloved Wife dies and Devoted Husband mourns." James, playing along, mimed tearful crying. "Time passes and Devoted Husband meets Potential Second

Wife. He finds himself caught between two forces: when he feels attracted to Potential Second, he immediately feels disloyal to the memory of Beloved. When he turns in devotion to Beloved, he feels he's being unfair to Potential Second. He feels like the rope in a tug-of-war." James mimed the role of the rope.

Angelica nodded. "I'm with you so far. But what's going on at the end of the story, when he starts acting like he wants a commitment from Potential Second, but he doesn't seem willing to make a commitment of his own?"

James stopped miming. "Yeah, what?"

"Well, again I'm just theorizing here—"

"Enough with the disclaimers. What's your theory?"

"I'd say Devoted Husband has made up his mind in principle. He wants to marry Potential Second and has set a goal to ask her. He just hasn't quite made it over the last hurdle, the one that will make it all real."

"Hmm," James said.

Angelica felt a shiver shoot down her spine. "You're right," she said, her voice firm. "That's exactly what's happening."

"Glad I could help." Heidi looked at James and shrugged.

"No, that's it. I feel certain." Angelica was beaming now. "All I have to do is be a little more patient. It's all going to work out just fine."

"I certainly hope so." Heidi's uncertainty was palpable.

"It's going to work out just fine," Joe told his sister as he herded his children out the door.

"I don't know about that," Cretia answered. "I'd almost bet she's expecting to see *you* at the airport, not you and the munchkins."

"I want her to feel included." Joe realized it sounded lame, but he wasn't quite at the point of telling his sister he hoped Angelica would feel like part of his family, that he wanted her to be. He was coming to the end of the longest two weeks he'd known in a while, and absence had only made him fonder. He still wasn't ready to spring a proposal on her—such things required timing and finesse—but he could hardly wait to see her again, and he wanted their evening to be perfect. He'd left the power plant in time to get showered and shaved before coming to get the kids. Now, if he timed things well, they'd get to the airport just before Angelica's plane touched down.

Joe had timed things perfectly, but he had not consulted the weather. A sudden dust storm near Sky Harbor had delayed the flight from Phoenix. By the time the plane landed nearly two hours later, Tori and Nick had had more than enough of the airport. Their whining had Joe on edge and other people in the terminal threatening to pay them to leave.

"Look, she's finally coming," Joe said as he watched the passengers debark. He pulled Nick away from the chair he was kicking. "Nick, try to remember some manners, will you?"

"I'm hungry," Nick whined.

"I know, I know. I promise we'll eat soon. Right now we're here to see Angelica. Remember how much you've missed her?"

Tori spoke up. "Yeah, Nicholas. Behave yourself."

Joe bit his tongue to avoid growling at Tori, who'd been no more pleasant than her brother.

Angelica came straggling in with the other bedraggled passengers. Her face fell when she saw them, and Joe realized it had been a tactical error to bring the kids, but his lovely lady rallied quickly. Inwardly, he thanked her for that. He stepped forward, greeting her with a quick hug and kiss. "Welcome home, beautiful."

"Hi," she answered. "Sorry my flight was late." She turned toward the children. "Hi, everyone."

"Welcome back, Angelica." Tori stepped forward with a tentative hug.

"Yeah, welcome back," Nick said, though he kept his distance and his look was anything but welcoming. "Dad, can we eat now?"

Joe was on the verge of snapping, but Angelica stepped forward and bent her knees, crouching in front of Nick so she met him eye-to-eye. "Are you tired of waiting?" she asked, her voice gentle.

"Yeah." Nick was petulant. "It took you a long time to get here."

"I know," Angelica said. "I'm tired, too. But I brought you something from Phoenix."

Nick's eyes widened. "You did?"

"Um-hm." She reached into her purse and brought out a plastic toy dinosaur a couple of inches high, still wrapped with a famous fast-food label.

"Wow! A Techno-saurus Rex!" Nick ripped the plastic off the toy and immediately started working the much-advertised "cranelike" jaw. Joe knew he'd wanted a "T-Rex" for weeks, but they were available only at one burger franchise, which had no outlets in their area. His heart swelled as he watched his son pacified by the woman he loved. He had no doubt Angelica was as weary and frustrated as any of the other passengers on the plane, or waiters in the terminal. Yet she was handling Nick with greater patience and wisdom than he had managed. His heart went out to her, and he promised himself that soon, very soon, he would ask her to marry him.

Angelica rose and turned toward Tori. "I have something for you, too," she said, putting her arm around his daughter, "but it's in my luggage."

"I don't mind waiting," Tori said. The look in her eyes was adoring, and Joe blessed once more the goodness that had brought this lovely woman into their lives.

"Come on," he said. "Let's get something to eat."

The lateness of the hour meant they went for fast food instead of the sit-down dinner Joe had planned, and it wasn't long before he was driving Angelica home. As they unloaded her luggage, she said, "One more thing. I have something special for Tori." Unzipping her garment bag, she produced violin sheet music and an autographed photo of one of the world's finest violinists, a man Tori idolized.

"You got . . . Oh, Angelica, thank you!" Tori flung herself into Angelica's arms, obviously overjoyed.

"I saw him play at Gammage Auditorium while I was in Phoenix."

"You saw him? Really?"

"Really. I'll tell you all about it, next lesson." She ruffled the girl's soft hair.

Joe hefted her luggage and walked her to her door, setting the bags inside. "Did you bring back anything for me?" he asked, trying to look as winsome as his children.

"Yes," Angelica said, mischief in her eyes, "but it's not in my luggage, and I didn't want to give it to you in front of the kids."

"Then I'm definitely sorry I brought the kids," he said. "Maybe tomorrow night? Can I take you to dinner, just the two of us?"

"I'd like that." Angelica stepped inside.

"I've missed you," Joe admitted, hesitant to let her go.

"I've missed you, too," she answered, and her brief good-night kiss was teeming with promises unfulfilled.

Thus the courtship began again. For most of the rest of August, Joe arranged to spend at least a little time each day, and most of every weekend, with Angelica. They ate almost every evening meal and went to every soccer game together. They talked about his work and Joe told her he was making connections and starting to feel more a part of the team. They took long walks and talked about problems with the children and how best to solve them, just as if they were already married. And neither of them mentioned that word.

On the Friday before school was to start, both children had special orientation programs at their school, and both adults arranged to take time away from work so they could be with first Nick, then Tori, at their schools. As they stood in front of the junior high school building where they'd first met, waiting for Tori to finish her tasks inside, Joe spoke. "It's been a long time, hasn't it?

"A long time and a lot of changes," Angelica answered.

"You know, there's something I've been wanting to talk to you about," Joe began, and Angelica thought, *Finally!*, but just then Tori came running out of the school with her P.E. uniform and locker combination in hand. Joe saw her coming and said, "How about a picnic tomorrow, just you and me?"

Angelica tried to look eager, rather than disappointed. "I'd love it," she said, "but I promised I'd help send out flyers about the soccer league startup. A bunch of us are getting together tomorrow at the McAllisters'."

Joe swallowed. "When do you think you'll be finished?"

"Too late for a picnic, I'd guess. We're starting just after noon, but the ladies decided we should send to families in Holbrook, too, so we have lots of flyers to mail. We're doing some organizational work as well. I'd guess we won't be done until dinnertime."

"Then have dinner with me?"

"Love to."

But it didn't work out that way. There was a problem with some of the flyers, and Angelica went with Eden Redhorse into town to have them recopied. She was also with her when Eden suddenly pulled her car off the highway and jumped out, violently ill.

"Are you all right?" Angelica asked in the aftermath, as she offered Eden some water from the thermos she'd found in the car.

"Yes," Eden answered, gasping in the warm, dry air.

"Forgive me, but you don't look all right. You look pale, and slightly . . . I don't know, sort of greenish."

Eden managed a wan smile. "My doctor tells me that's normal in the first trimester."

"Eden, you're pregnant!"

Eden nodded.

"Congratulations!" Angelica gave her a heartfelt, if gentle, hug.

"Thanks, but please don't mention anything when we get back to the other ladies. Logan and I aren't ready to tell other people yet. Besides, I want to be careful how

I say it around Sarah, since she's my best friend in the world and she can't have children of her own."

"She can't?" Angelica, who had often wondered whether she would ever have children, felt that pain clear to her toes.

Eden shook her head. "You knew Sarah was married and widowed before she met Chris. . . ."

"I hadn't heard."

"Well, she was. She was carrying a baby when her husband died."

"How did he—? I'm sorry. I shouldn't ask."

"It's okay," Eden answered. "He was a rodeo cowboy. He died trying to ride a bull named Widowmaker."

"Ironic." Angelica felt her throat tightening.

"Yeah. Anyway, Sarah lost her baby a few weeks later, and there were complications. Her doctors said she'll probably never conceive again."

Angelica digested all that information as she walked Eden back to the car. With it came the knowledge that *she* wanted children, desperately, that she'd even like to try the process of natural motherhood, sickness in the middle of the afternoon and all. Realizing Eden was waiting for some kind of response to her revelation, she said, "Don't worry. I won't tell anyone about this little incident, and I'm sure Sarah will be happy for you when she hears."

"I hope so," Eden answered. They drove back toward the farm.

"Well, you two took long enough," Meg greeted them when they got back to the McAllister farm. The unplanned errand, complete with its unplanned stop, had taken much longer than anyone had guessed. Then they kept running into other problems that slowed them down:

Meg kept leaving the room at odd moments; Sarah disappeared a little after four and was found napping on the couch; Alexa had a half-dozen long phone calls come in, most of which she took in the other room. Around 4:30, Angelica quipped to Cretia that they were the only two who seemed able to stay with the schedule. That's when Cretia said, "You're on your own for a little while" and vanished for a full half-hour. Though Angelica had promised to meet Joe at six, by 5:30 it was clear they wouldn't be done by six, or probably even by seven.

"I'm sorry," she told him when she called. "It looks like we had more work here than we knew. I'd guess it will be closer to eight before we finish."

"I'm sorry, too," Joe said, then there was a long silence. "How about tomorrow? We can take a picnic into the hills after church."

"We already promised everyone we'd come to the potluck here tomorrow—"

"I know, but let's get out of it. I'll go out right now and buy a couple of prepared dishes, and we'll drop those and the kids with Max and Cretia before we take off on our own."

"Joe, I—"

"Please? There's something I want to talk to you about."

"Well, in that case . . ." Angelica was still smiling when she went back to the other women.

They sat together in church again, but by now everyone was so used to seeing them together that not even Irene Duncan seemed eager to gossip. Joe, finally tired of waiting for the "right time," had decided to make one of his own. Yes, it was a big step to ask a woman to share his life. He knew that now even better than he had when he'd proposed to Roberta. But it was time—past time, in fact. He wanted Angelica for his own, he wanted her as part of his life and his family, and he didn't want to wait a minute longer than necessary to make it happen.

As soon as the benediction was spoken and the post-lude music began, Joe hustled his children into Max and Cretia's van, said quick good-byes, and drove Angelica out of town to a place he'd selected on a bluff over-looking the town, not far from the place where he'd last chatted with his late wife, and had persuaded himself that she would approve of his plans to remarry.

He pulled the car to a stop and set the emergency brake, then he spread a blanket and brought out the pic-nic basket. "Hungry?" he asked as he spread the meal.

"No, I think I'd rather talk first." Angelica's expres-sion was pleasant, but he couldn't help noticing her voice was tight.

Is she anticipating what I'm going to say? he won-dered. *Isn't she happy about it?* "Was there something special you wanted to talk about?"

She tossed her hair and he was reminded of what a splendid-looking woman he was proposing to, yet her voice was even tighter when she answered, "You said you wanted to talk."

"That I did." He cleared his throat. "You know the kids both start school tomorrow. . . ."

Angelica waited, then said, "Yes."

"Then the following weekend is the Labor Day holiday."

"Yes."

"I was just . . . wondering whether you have plans for Labor Day."

Angelica's eyes flashed with something that looked very much like anger, and Joe saw the rosy tinge of a blush rising on her throat. "Not yet."

This wasn't going as Joe had planned. He decided to try another tack. "When you have a big musical recital in your home, how many people can you accommodate?"

The rosy flush spread all the way to her hairline and her lovely sky eyes turned stormy. "Joe Vanetti, is that what you brought me up here to talk about—Labor Day holidays and musical recitals? Because if that's it, you can turn around and take me home right now." She stood, towering above him like some Norse goddess, hands on her hips, golden hair flowing behind her in the breeze.

He grinned. "You're magnificent, you know that? Stunning, in fact."

"Joe, really . . ."

He stood, too. "I just thought maybe . . . If you'll wait just a minute . . ."

Angelica's patience gave way all at once. "I'm *tired* of waiting! I'm thirty-three years old, Joe, and unlike you and almost everyone else I know, I've never been married. I've never even had a serious boyfriend. And I want that, Joe Vanetti! I want a beautiful wedding and a romantic honeymoon and a baby of my own. I want to throw up in the middle of the afternoon because I'm pregnant, and to have dark circles under my eyes because I've been up walking a fussy infant, and to get called in from work to meet with the principal in her office because my son or daughter is in trouble at school. I want all of it, and I don't want to *wait* any longer. So if you're not going to get around to—"

"Whoa! Whoa!" He stepped toward her as if to take her in his arms. "Wow. I've never seen you angry before."

She stepped back. "I've never felt so provoked before." She seemed only slightly mollified. "I've never done violence to a human being, either, but if you say another word about Labor Day or recitals—"

"I understand." Joe stared in admiration at the most magnificent woman he had ever seen as he held up his hands in a gesture of truce. "This isn't going the way I'd planned it," he said. "Tell you what: Will you just stand right there for a second?" He caught her expression as she started to speak. "Just a second, honest. Okay?

She didn't answer, but closed her lips and tipped her head back in a defiant look that said, *We'll see.*

During the two weeks when Angelica had been in Phoenix, Joe had scoured the jewelry stores. He'd visited practically every store in northeastern Arizona, looking for exactly the right ring—something simple yet elegant, beautiful but rare, something like his Angelica. He'd finally found it in a small corner shop in Winslow. Now he reached into the pocket of his jeans and brought out the jeweler's box. He opened it to display the ring before her, a two-carat marquise-cut diamond in a leaflike spray of smaller stones. Dropping to one knee before her, he took her hand in his. "Angelica DeForest, will you marry me?"

Her eyes went wide. "What?"

"Marry me," he said again. "Let's have a beautiful wedding and a romantic honeymoon. I hadn't planned on having more children, but if you want a baby, we can do that, too. I want you for my wife, Angelica, and as a second mother to my son and daughter. I want you as my companion for the rest of my life. Please say yes."

Tears pooled in her eyes and began to run down her cheeks as Angelica knelt, too, taking Joe's hand. "Oh, Joe . . . I thought you'd never ask!"

"It's only been a couple of months," he said, sliding the ring onto her finger.

"It's been twenty-two years," she corrected, wiping tears from her face. She held the ring before her, admiring it. "It's so beautiful!"

"You're so beautiful," he said, and took her in his arms.

Their kiss was long and tender, replete with promises made and kept, commitments stretching far into the future. When they finally separated, Joe asked, "I assume that's a yes?"

Angelica pursed her lips, then smiled sweetly as she answered, "Yes. But can I ask what all that nonsense about musical recitals was about?"

"I thought maybe we could be married on Labor Day," Joe said, "in your house."

"*Our* house," she said, "but that soon?"

"As you've pointed out so aptly, we've waited long enough."

"It takes a little longer than that to plan a wedding, Joe."

"How long?"

"With help, luck, and blessings, at least six or seven weeks."

"Then we'll plan for a Saturday in early October. I don't want to wait a minute longer, though we may have to wait for a honeymoon trip. I doubt if I can take time off this soon."

"I won't mind," she answered, eyes flashing. "It will be a honeymoon, if we're together."

Joe decided that answer deserved a kiss. Some time later, he said, "Well, are you ready for lunch now?"

Angelica shook her head. "Let's tell the kids instead. We can take this food as part of the potluck. We'll call the kids out and tell them what we're planning, then we can make our announcement to the McAllister clan."

"Good idea," Joe agreed. "Seeing the way they got behind the soccer league, they may just be able to help us pull off a wedding sooner than you imagined."

"You're right," she said. "They probably could." She helped him pack up the picnic and they drove toward the farm.

"Well, well, the gang's all here," Kate announced as they entered the front door. Angelica looked around and saw it was true. Kate and Wiley were there, sitting with Joan and Bob and their children. Jim, Meg and Alexis were sharing a table with Kurt and Alexa, Chris and Sarah, Logan and Eden. Max and Cretia sat at another table with Nick and Tori, Lydia and Danny, and Max's daughter Marcie, who had come back from California for the new school year.

"I guess we're rounding out the group," Angelica said. "If you folks will excuse us, we'd like to talk with Tori and Nick for a minute."

Knowing looks went around the room as the children left their seats and the door closed behind them. Joe led his family away from the house to get some privacy. As he started to speak, Nick asked, "So is Angelica going to marry us?" Angelica responded with startled laughter, then they all laughed and celebrated for a moment before going back for the public announcement.

They stepped into the great room of the McAllister home, and Joe said, "Hey, everybody! We have an announcement."

"It's about time!" Meg said, and everyone laughed.

"Don't you even want to hear what it is?" Angelica asked.

"We already know what," Cretia said. "All we need to hear is when."

Joe grinned. "As soon as possible," he said. "We thought maybe you movers and shakers could help us make it happen."

"No problem," Kate said.

"I'll do the cake," Cretia volunteered.

"My gown would probably fit you," Eden said to Angelica, "unless you really want one of your own."

"The local printer owes me a favor," Kurt said. "I bet we can have your invitations done in record time."

"Whoa! Whoa, everybody!" It was Jim. "The planning can hold for a moment. Right now, I'd say congratulations are in order." He raised his water glass. "A toast to the happy couple."

"Hear-hear," Wiley chimed in, raising his glass also. The extended family toasted the new couple with ice-water and strawberry soda. When they finished cheering, Wiley said, "It seems to be the day for announcements. You just missed Logan and Eden's."

"We're having a baby," Logan announced, and everyone cheered again.

"When are you due, Eden?" Meg asked.

"Around the ides of March," Eden answered.

"Mid-March, huh?" Meg answered. "Your baby will

be about two weeks younger than ours. We're due the first of the month."

"Meg!" Kate cried. "Congratulations!" And there was another round of cheers and good wishes.

"Well, it seems to be the day for announcements," Kurt said. He turned a speaking look toward his wife.

Alexa smiled. "I think he wants me to tell you that I've been offered a post as head screenwriter for the new Andrew Kleeson production." A respectful hush fell over the room. "But I've turned it down," she added. "I'm taking a backup position instead."

"Why on earth would you—" Kate began. "That is, unless—"

"Our baby is due in late February," Kurt announced, and the cheers and toasts went around again.

"Well," Max said. "I guess it's our turn. Not to be outdone . . ."

"You're having a baby, too?" Tori asked.

Lydia answered, "Danny wants a brother, but Marcie and I are voting for a girl."

"We're due in April," Cretia finished.

Another round of congratulations followed, then Marcie said, "Gee, it looks like everybody is preg—" She stopped when she saw her father gesturing wildly. The room grew silent as family members guiltily glanced in the direction of Chris and Sarah.

Sarah stood. "It's all right."

"Oh, Sarah," Eden said, her voice heavy with apology.

Then Sarah said, "No really, Eden. It's all right. We agreed not to say anything until we were past the risky stages, but . . ." She looked to her husband.

"We're ahead of all of you," Chris announced. "Our baby is due around Valentine's Day."

"Oh, Sarah! That's wonderful!" people cried. The cheers were even louder and more heartfelt as the family congratulated Chris and Sarah on the conception that was never expected to happen. When the din quieted, Kate spoke. "I always knew this house would be filled with grandchildren one day. I'm glad I'm here to see it."

"So are we, Mom," Chris said, and the assembled family agreed.

"But I fear we've shorted Joe and Angelica of their celebration," Kate went on. "With all our other happy announcements, we've rather drowned them out."

"We'll make it up to them," Alexa said. "Anything this family sets its collective mind to gets done. We'll have them happily married in a month."

"That soon?" Angelica asked.

"It only took three weeks for us," Wiley said.

"Wonderful," she answered.

Joe put his arm around her in a possessive gesture. "Now if you folks will excuse us for a minute," he said, "I'd like to celebrate with my fiancée alone?" Amid the cheers and catcalls, he led Angelica onto the porch, held her close, and asked, "What do you think? Are you still glad you said yes?"

"More so every minute." She kissed him.

"Angelica?"

"Yes, love?"

"You remember that day early in the summer when you told me you'd once wanted to be called Angie, but you didn't feel like an Angie anymore?"

She nodded. "I remember."

"I told you then that you needed a nickname. Well, I have one for you, but it's going to be just between us, okay?"

She wrinkled her nose. "Even if I hate it?"

"You won't hate it."

"Okay, try me."

"Angel," he said. "You're my saving Angel."

She smiled, dawn breaking over the desert. "I could get used to that."

He kissed her, long and thoroughly, then opened the door. "Come on, Angel. Let's get back to the family."